ACCORDING TO…

ACCORDING TO...

By

Diana Jeanne

Published by Taylor-Dth Publishing
108 Caribe Isle,
Novato, CA 94949

WWW.TAYLOR-DTH.COM

ISBN: 978-0-9834780-2-7

Manufactured in the United States of America

To my family and friends
who support my endeavor.

Edited by Rhonda Moffett

Cover design by Nathalie Rose

According To . . .

In the beginning God created the heavens.
Out of the light the Angels were born.
Out of the darkness the demons grew.
Then God created the Earth,
And from the creatures of light and darkness,
God created Man,
And he saw it was good.

Chapter One

I was the dreamer, although not always asleep. No matter what, the dreams kept coming.

We all dream whether we want to or not. These were not those dreams. The ones where you awaken, but within seconds you can no longer recall what the dreams were about. These dreams were burned into my soul and I could not dispose of them.

I had a life before they started. I was born in Boise, Idaho. I was the seventh child of seven girls. I did all the things girls did: tee-ball, girl scouts, drama club.

My parents paid for most things, but lap tops and cell phones we paid for with our own money.

With the help of grants, we all went to college. I earned a degree in psychology, and moved to White Fish Point in Michigan. Helping troubled children work through different issues was my purpose, and it was very rewarding to me.

Although I had no friends or family there, initially, the people soon regarded me as one of their own. The view of Lake Superior in the morning was beautiful. I loved my ride to work.

All was well in the world of Ana, until that first night and that first dream.

I sold my home and my practice. Now I live in a sanctuary named the Lighthouse, working for free room and board. I take only what I must from my savings for food. There are hundreds of people outside these walls waiting to catch a glimpse of me.

The dreams have consumed my life. I am debilitated by them. I sit day in and day out writing them down. I did not ask for this. I just want them to stop, but I have no control over what is happening.

I remember that first night. It was the seventh day of the seventh month of the year 2032. I finished working in the garden. After a quick dinner and a few TV shows, I headed off to sleep. It seemed to me my eyes had just closed, when I was awakened in a dream.

I dreamt I was flying over Lake Superior and looking down on the town of White Fish Point. I was dressed in a white gown.

That first night I did not see anyone around me. In the distance I saw a light of orange and white descending onto a city. It seemed so far away, and yet I knew it was Detroit. It was like something nuclear, but it wasn't a nuclear bomb. It was something else. The closer I flew to it, the more I saw.

Inside the light was an angel with outstretched white wings. His body was covered in long golden robes. His eyes were burned out and blackened. His face looked flattened, and he had short white hair.

He stood at least twenty feet tall, and a sword was tethered around his waist.

I don't know if he saw me, because his face never changed from its flat affect.

Engulfed in the light he descended into the city.

When his feet touched the ground I heard the screams of women. It was a wailing that only comes from deep within a woman's body when her children are butchered before her eyes. The wailing seemed to resonate throughout the city.

The majestic angel spread his arms, and a cold, freezing air descended from the heavens. It spread across the land.

The freezing cold did not differentiate between man and beast. Dead birds fell from the trees by the thousands, frozen. Dogs, cats, rats and mice all succumbed to the cold. Homeless people who unwittingly stayed out of the shelters were frozen in seconds.

Then the angel sheathed his sword, and in an instant he was gone.

I beheld another angel. A female. She was dressed in black robes, layered, looking like silk. Her hair was long and white. Her eyes were burned out like those of the angel before her. When she landed on the ground, a black aura surrounded her sandals. The blackness spread from the sidewalks to the streets, and throughout the city.

The wailing created by the first angel softened to cries and moans. The people fled from inside their homes to the streets, frantically trying to escape their inevitable, unknown fate.

I focused on one of the people; a tall, man who was heavy set. He wore green pajama pants and white socks with no shoes. He held a blue bandana over his mouth. He stopped suddenly in the middle of the street as though his body seized, went semi-rigid for a few seconds, then coughed. He dropped the bandana. Blood poured from every orifice in his body. His knees buckled and he fell to the ground, making a gurgling sound.

More people emerged from their homes. They were slain. The streets ran red with blood as bodies fell, one on top of another. It was a sea of death. There was no escape for any of them. The streets of the city became an open grave.

I flew over the whole area. In my mind I cataloged the devastation. I saw them as they lay, bleeding to death.

A young black girl with long curly hair caught my attention. As I watched her gasping her final breath, with the blood running down her face, a light hit me. It was only for a second, and suddenly I was in an alley. It was early morning. The smell from a nearby green trash can was disgusting. I moved a little closer. No one seemed to be able to see me.

There, in the alley, was the black woman. She wore a Lani Barten outfit with a Farana purse. She was speaking with a boy no more than twelve or thirteen years old. His hands shook as he spoke to her.

"Please, I only got twenty seven dollars. I'll bring ya three more dollars tomorrow. I need to get my sick off," he said, pleading with her.

"Okay," she said. "But you will get no more from me without the money." She handed him three small packets of white powder. "You're lucky I like you," she said, grabbing the money.

The well dressed woman walked out of the alley and got into a black Mercedes Benz.

My vision returned to the alley, where the boy sat with his eyes rolled up in his head, and with his brown, worn, leather belt strapped around his arm for a tourniquet, with a used needle and syringe hanging from the vein in his arm.

I saw him die, alone, in a stinking alley, where no one would miss him.

Suddenly, I was back above the streets, watching as the girl breathed her last.

Then I was flying over the city. Detroit became a cesspool over the last ten years. No one worked, and everyone lived off the government. The designer drug, called PNT, sucked in the young, and younger children. They died from drug use.

I looked across the city and saw no life anywhere, no sounds except for a lingering agonal breath. There was nothing more.

I felt conflicted about that one girl's death.

Looking up, I saw a third angel. He landed gently on the ground. His hair was black and his skin was black. His eyes were white, as if he wore a white mask. He wore a long flowing white gown that sparkled as he moved. His wings were black and beautiful, and with his wings spread, he was magnificent to behold, with his feet covered by sandals.

A tear rolled down my right cheek in response to the vision of this angel.

The ground opened, and hundreds of sparrows flew from inside the earth, singing an amazing melody, a cacophony of sound as they rose into the sky, flying straight up, disappearing into the clouds.

The angel opened his arms, and brought a wall of fire all around him. He pushed the fire outward, and it engulfed the city.

Everything burned, except for a blue building in the center of the city. In all the destruction, it stood unharmed.

Then, from where the birds came, I saw what looked like lava. It acted like a virus. It ate the cement and the remnants of the buildings until all that was left was a black tar over the entire area of Detroit. It looked as though Detroit never existed. The smell was putrid and the sight horrific, yet I could not look away.

I wept for the people. I wept for the children. I wept, because in a large city like Detroit, there was no one left to save.

Tears rolled down my cheeks.

I saw the third angel sheathe his sword and disappear.

Looking up, I saw a man across from me suspended in the air wearing the same white robe I wore. His hair was sandy blond and his eyes were blue. He was like me, in his twenties.

Our eyes met, and I wanted to say something to him, but could not make my mouth move.

I needed to find him to talk to him. Maybe he could tell me what I am supposed to do with this information.

My memory flashed on the story of Sodom and Gomorrah, when Abraham asked God, "If there were a hundred good people, would He spare the city?" Abraham actually got God to agree to spare the city if there were only ten people.

But in all of Detroit there was no one worth saving.

I beheld a large man, fifteen feet tall. He was a brown skinned man with no face and black, straw like hair. Out of his abdomen grew seven green snakes with bald baboon heads and overly large incisor teeth that fitted perfectly next to one another. There was a red ring where the snakes connected to the abdomen. And in the red rings there were twelve black stars. The seven heads made an awful screeching sound as their mouths opened and closed.

The man wore brown leather pants, and carried a raw hide whip that he cracked next to the baboon heads to drive them in the right direction. He moved them through Detroit, consuming people on the way, heading for Toledo, Ohio. When he reached the outskirts of the city, he stopped, as if waiting for something.

That was when I saw a star falling to earth.

I heard a voice crying out to open the ocean for the star to be buried within the ocean's floor.

The ocean did open, and the star crashed into the ocean floor, producing a light so bright it blinded me for a second. It looked like lightning rose from the ocean.

A wall of water rose from the depths of the ocean and crashed onto the coast of California. The water drowned anyone within a mile of the coast, as they lay asleep in their beds, dreaming their own dreams.

I wondered if they had any warning. What good are dreams if they cannot protect you?

I felt my body being pulled backward. Streaks of light surrounded me. I felt myself slam back into my body.

I woke up screaming and crying. My hands shook as I tried to rise from my bed. I was so weakened, I had trouble standing or walking. I managed to get to the kitchen sink, where I drew a glass of water. I knelt in front of the sink, drinking the water as fast as I could. I was so thirsty that one glass was not enough. After my third glass of water, I dropped to the floor and lay down. The cold tile floor felt so good on my cheek. My head pounded. I breathed heavily. Even if I wanted to get up, my legs would not support me. I learned what 'weak as a kitten' meant.

Looking across the floor, I noticed some dust bunnies hiding under the cabinets and dishwasher. I reminded myself that when I felt better, I would have to sweep the floors.

I couldn't tell myself I was just dreaming, for I wasn't! I looked at the clock, and saw it was almost six in the morning. I had one hour left for sleeping, but I chose not to sleep. As far as I was concerned, I would not be sleeping ever again.

After a very long shower while shedding a lot of tears, I got dressed for work, putting on my blue, silk one piece uniform. While sitting to eat my breakfast, I noticed a pain that started from inside my brain, moving outward. I heard a low alarm, but was unsure where it came from. I shut off the TV and my laptop, and went from electronic device to electronic device to locate the source of the alarm, but couldn't.

Since the alarm was not coming from anything in the house, my next move was to go outside.

There was no change in the alarm.

Opening and closing my mouth or holding my ears closed did not make a difference. The sound was not going away, so I returned inside, and sat at the kitchen table.

"I can't go to work like this," I said to myself. I retrieved my appointment book, and called Sara, my first client for the day.

Sara was eighteen, and I worked with her for the last two years. She was raped by her father when she turned thirteen. Her mother was ill with multiple sclerosis. For a whole two years, her mother pretended not to know what was wrong with her daughter.

The problem lasted until the school called one day, and Sara was taken away. Her mother divorced her father, and as a stipulation of the court's ruling, Sara needed to see a therapist three times a week.

"Sara," I said

"Yes," she replied

"I won't be in today," I told her

"Okay, but why are you yelling?" she asked

"Sorry about that," I said. "Bye"

"Bye," she replied.

I got a yellow pad of paper, and sat at the table to write. "July 7, 2023. The dream..."

My head stopped hurting and the ringing alarm ceased. Raising the pen, I waited. The pain started again. When I resumed writing, the pain receded.

The words flowed like water from my pen, as if something took possession of me. It took me over an hour to write down the dream. Afterward, I felt physically and emotionally drained.

I brushed back tears, and went to the bathroom. Combing back my light brown hair, I looked into the mirror. I saw circles under my dark brown eyes. The two things my mother said she gave me at birth were good looks and a great faith. I wondered why God was showing me these things! I kept thinking about Jonah, and how he ran from God.

When I read the story I thought, why would anyone run away from God? I laughed aloud at the idea of anyone running from God.

I looked more closely in the mirror. I noticed the soft blond highlights in my hair.

"How do you like that?" I said to myself. No need to visit the cosmetologist. I could save the money.

I decided to take the day off. I went online and searched web sites where people wrote they believed the Apocalypse was coming.

Had my eyes been closed? I wondered. I had dismissed these people as nuts, never realizing that the nuts became mainstream.

The Apocalypse was big business, too. Almost

every web site sold meal rations, back up generators, large water containers, ham radios and gas masks. I had the irrational feeling that I should be stocking up on these things.

I remembered what Brother Antonio used to say to us in church. "If the world is ending, it means that Jesus is returning. So when that day comes, we must tell ourselves, 'God, we are ready'. It was the smartest thing I heard. Even at the time, I thought there must be a few people pressuring him to address the issue.

I thought of every book I saw. I turned off, or turned away from every talk show on TV, but the thoughts returned. The end was coming, and I had closed my eyes to it, to not see it.

When I took a trip to Los Angeles for a conference, there was a tall black man by the old Hollywood Walk of Fame. He was telling people the end was coming. He wore tattered jeans and a red shirt. He was dirty and emaciated, with a hoarse voice. I got a bottle of water to give to him, but I was unsure whether he would see me or respond to me. My initial thought was that the poor man had schizophrenia.

People would move away from him, or look away. No one really wanted to see him. I slowly handed him the water. He clenched onto my arm saying, "May God bless you."

He opened the bottled water and drank it in about a minute. As I slowly walked away, I wondered if there was something more I could have done. Perhaps I should have asked him when he last ate. I could have helped him.

I pulled out a second yellow pad. Paper and pens are expensive, now, because everything is done online, but I liked the feeling of holding a pen in my hand and writing on a piece of paper. I started writing the names of different companies I visited online.

I talked online to a nice guy from an online store called Apocalypse Now, who had a full line of items for the end of the world. I asked him all the pertinent questions. When I asked him when this would happen, his reply was, "Soon!"

When I pressed him for more specifics, he said he did not have time. He had to get ready for the comic book convention. I found that rather amusing.

It was after two p.m. when I finally rose from my chair, feeling like I had a vast knowledge of all the internet sites.

The grumbling in my neglected stomach made me opt for an early dinner. After a large and scrumptious meal, I decided I needed to go to the source, so I sat with my kindle and read the book of Revelation according to John. I was a good Catholic girl, because my mother would sit with me and my sisters at night to read the bible to us. That was something I would never forget.

When we were young, she read Children Bible stories to us. The older we became, the more she used the actual bible.

When I was fourteen my father was in a car accident. My mom and all seven of us girls stood around his bed and prayed the Rosary. His recovery, according to the doctors, was miraculous!

When my grandmother died my mother told us, regardless of how much we loved her it was her time to go and be in the arms of Jesus.

When I made my confirmation, I chose my mom as my sponsor. She actually cried.

Returning my thoughts to the present, I wondered if I should call her, although I knew to do so would cause her undue worry and anxiety. I decided to keep my thoughts to myself.

I reread Revelation, and was amazed at the symbolism. That is what my mother told me would happen.

Perhaps the dream was just that, although it certainly did not seem like symbolism. What if it were real? I needed help. I couldn't call my parents or my sisters, it would only worry them. If the dream recurred, then I would go for help.

I felt very close to Brother Antonio, at our parish, who was on sabbatical. If my dreaming did not go stop, I would go see him. I was a Eucharist Minister at the 9:30 mass, through that effort, I came to know him.

"I'll see if the dream recurs," I said aloud, as if saying it aloud would make it not happen.

I tried to find a similarity between my angels and John's angels. So far there was not too much there.

I needed to move. Sitting in one place too long made me stiff. I stood, and stretched, then went into the bathroom. I splashed cold water on my face, and dried off with a blue hand towel. Looking into the mirror, I saw a younger version of my mother. At twenty four I was a very pretty woman, with brown hair, with highlights, large brown eyes and olive complexion. I was five feet eight with a pear shape.

I dated several men, but no one seriously. Yet, if it were the end of the world, then I would have regrets for not experiencing womanhood.

I did not marry, nor have children. I would have liked to be a mother, to maybe have a little girl or boy of my own. I wiped a stray tear away with my hand. Such a silly thought. Who says the world is ending, anyway?

After a quick grilled cheese sandwich, I sat down to watch TV. My mind was on overload, and TV was the best cure for that condition. It was nine fifteen and I could barely keep my eyes open, but I didn't want to fall asleep.

I pulled myself off my black leather couch, and headed to my bedroom. After changing into my flannel pj's, I knelt at my bedside. I prayed to God, as I do every day, and thanked Jesus for the many blessings I had in my life. However, I had not actually knelt by my bed to pray since I was a little girl.

The prayer unconsciously ran through my mind. "Now I lay me down to sleep I pray the Lord my soul to keep, If I should die before I wake, I pray the Lord my soul to take." It seemed a fitting prayer.

I shook my head and continued praying, "Please, God. I am not sure I am the right person for these dreams. Maybe the dreams should go to someone with political powers or extreme faith. I am just Ana, no one special. I sighed deeply.

"I should know by now that is not your style,"

I continued. "Please help me understand what I am supposed to do. In your name I pray, Amen." I climbed into my tall bed, settled under the covers and was soon fast asleep.

I dreamt I was flying again. The tall man with no face and seven green snakes attached to his abdomen was moving from the south of Detroit to Toledo, Ohio. He cracked the brown whip on either side of the bald baboon snake heads, changing their direction to suit his needs. I could clearly see the red rings where the snakes attached to the man's abdomen. The twelve black stars remained on the red connections.

The snake creatures ate everything in their path; people, animals and birds. They left crushed homes and blood splatter in their wake.

Everyone was sleeping. As they awoke to the screams of their neighbors, they could not move fast enough to get away. The teeth of the snakes were gruesome. The mouths of the snakes were full of incisor teeth. Their jaws were strong enough to snap bones in half.

I watched as husbands tried to save their wives or children. The result was always the same.

I wanted to look away, but realized there might be clues or information there that I could use to change what I saw. Perhaps I could go to Detroit and warn the people there of the impending doom.

I could wear sackcloth like the people of Nineveh, I thought, but, I don't think I have sackcloth in my wardrobe. I don't think I even know what sackcloth looks like, but I could improvise.

I was having this whole conversation in my

brain while all this destruction was happening. Oh my God, I said to myself. I should be thinking about these poor people and not about sackcloth.

Looking down, I watched the man with no face cut a twenty mile path across Detroit to the South Suburbs and towards Toledo.

Suddenly, I saw movement just outside the path of destruction. Neighbors, friends and Christians were coming to the scene and looking through the rubble to find survivors.

My heart lifted. I knew our country was made of altruistic people. I knew there was good with the bad. I could change this evil destruction some how, some way. That is why I was made to be a witness.

I looked across from me to see a young man. He was about my age, dressed in a long white gown.

He opened his mouth to speak.

I watched closely.

"Levi James" he said in introduction.

I forced my head to shake up and down to let him know I heard him. It was very draining just to do that.

My eyes returned back to the man. His black straw-like hair was unmoved. He had a slit in his face for breathing, but nothing else: no eyes, no mouth, no nose, just the slit. The snakes must be his eyes and the people they consumed must feed him, I thought. How else would he know which way to go?

The bald baboon snake heads were spread out. That was how they could create a swath of destruction twenty miles across.

At one point, I saw a very large man running

from one snake and right into the path of the other. The two snakes cut him in half as if he were a snack. They hissed at each other, afterward.

The man slapped his brown rawhide whip between the two of them. A blue electrical light crashed out of the whip. Two snakes winced and retreated.

I saw a great light. It came from the stars and stood in front of me. Inside the light I saw Jesus, our Lord and Savior. He was magnificent and more beautiful than any soul I ever encountered.

I forced myself to my knees. I felt ashamed for the many indiscretions I committed in my life.

He took my hand, and pulled me up.

For a minute that seemed to last forever, I saw into my Savior's eyes. His soft hand cupped my face as tears of joy rolled down my cheeks. He leaned in so close to me I thought he was going to kiss my face. He whispered into my ear and floated away.

I was stunned. A feeling of great peace came over me, a peace like I never felt before. I called out to him in my mind. "Don't leave me, Christ. Please." But he disappeared in the stars.

I remember learning from the writings of Saint Augustine that hell was living in the absence of, or without the presence of God. I understood that all too well, now.

I was flying again, following the man with the seven green snakes. The lights ahead of me told me I was heading into Toledo. I wondered why Christ came only to me and gave me the message he did. I thought that I could die this night because I saw my

Savior, and my heart soared.

I saw the man with no face stop before the city limits of Toledo. A star fell to the earth, and I heard a voice command the ocean to open.

To my amazement, I watched as the wall of water washed over the people on the coast of California.

I saw the first angel again appear over the city of Toledo, surrounded by an orange and white light. When he landed in the city, I heard the cries of the mothers losing their babies.

The angel was bathed in light with his golden robes rustling about his majestic body. The sound his movement invoked was so guttural, as thousands of mother's made the sound. They did not have to rise from their sleep, they simply knew inside their souls what was happening.

I looked closer at the angel bathed in light, at his white hair and fair complexion. I wondered why his eyes were burned out. Perhaps it was better he could not see what was happening. There were letters on the pleats of his golden robes. I tried to remember them. He spread out his white wings and arms in a single movement, startling me.

I beheld the cold. It spread out from his sandal clad feet.

I saw teenage boys, playing basketball, freeze and fall over dead. The birds fell from the trees and the skies in record number. I heard the whimpers of dogs and cats as they died.

The homeless outside turned to sheets of ice. The first angel sheathed his sword. He was surrounded by fire and then disappeared.

The second angel appeared. I could tell she was a female by her figure, although I was unsure of this the first time I saw her.

She was covered in black silk robes that flowed as she moved.

I saw the white light as she descended into the city of Toledo.

I yelled, "Stop! No, please!"

My words had no effect on the angel. Her white wings spread out. She had white hair longer than the first angel's, and her eyes were black and burned out.

The ground shook as her massive body touched down. Darkness spread from beneath her robes, into the city. The cries of the people turned to moans as they rushed out of their homes.

Death took them all. Blood ran from their every orifice, the blood became a river; a river of blood that coursed down the icy streets until there was no asphalt or concrete untouched by it.

Were they all sinners, all unworthy, even the children? What terrible thing had they committed against God that He should plight them so? After all, we were Americans. We did not blow up bus loads of children. God was in our money and on our declaration. God was in our hearts and in our souls. Were there not ten people in the city of Toledo or in the city of Los Angeles who could have been saved?

The pain in my chest was ferocious. I was moving toward the angel. There were clouds around me, as if there to protect me.

"Stop!" I yelled.

The angel did not respond.

I moved forward, and I suddenly realized the ground was coming up quickly.

"I can't be hurt. I'm dreaming," my mind reminded me.

"Oh, crap," I said, when I saw the dead people lying all over the ground, eyes wide open; dead eyes starring at the heavens, begging for redemption. There were no exceptions; no race, no creed, no color, no age, no discrimination.

The pain in my chest increased. I reached for the people. The clouds that protected me were gone as the ground rushed up to meet me.

I felt arms around my waist, pulling me backward. Strong male arms were protecting me. I was soon back in the clouds, looking down at the destruction.

I faced him, the owner of those arms. They belonged to Levi.

"Levi," I said, recognizing him.

He smiled at me. He was a great looking guy. I wouldn't kick him to the curb, I thought, smiling. I realized it was the first time I smiled since all of this started.

We were pulled apart by unseen forces. The next thing I heard was the sound of unseen trumpets coming from all around me.

I saw a great beast. It rose out of the smoke in the ruins of Toledo. It was ten feet tall. Its name was Extinction. I heard the name in my head. It had six clawed legs as black as coal. It looked like a tarantula.

The way it walked was similar to a spider, but it had the head of a goat, with horns and long snout.

It had large pustules on its face and body, draining everywhere. The draining pus would start fires wherever they landed as it walked in the city of Toledo.

It stopped to snack on the dead bodies.

I watched intently as it came to a very pregnant woman who wore a short red dress. Using its black claws, it ripped open the woman's abdomen and pulled the fetus from the mother's womb. I'm sure I heard a cry as the creature bit off the head of the unprotected infant. I had to turn away from this gruesome sight.

I looked up, and saw an angel coming toward me. She was different than the others. She stood before me in a white flowing gown with blond hair and eyes of sapphire blue. Her white, extended wings were meticulously clean and bright. When she spoke, the sound resonated around me.

"Fear not, my child," she said "I will hold back the destruction until all the signs have come to pass. There is little time to waste, for the signs have already started."

She reached out her hand to me. I saw my arm raise, although not of my own accord. When she touched my hand, I felt as though I was being electrocuted.

Then I saw images inside my brain. They were coming so fast that I was overwhelmed.

"Please. Wait," I begged her.

I heard screaming. I was being pulled back

to my bed. I awoke still screaming. My right hand throbbing in pain. I raised my arm, but the pain only intensified.

On my palm was a circular burn with stars. I struggled out of bed, and with one hand, crawled to the kitchen. I pulled myself up to turn on the faucet and stick my hand under the water.

Smoke rose from the water, where it touched my hand.

The images continued running through my brain, like a movie I couldn't stop watching. I lay my face against the top of the sink, leaving my hand under the cold water. My whole body hurt as though I had been pummeled by an unseen force.

I must have fallen asleep for a short time. When I awoke, I was still hanging over the kitchen sink.

I had a terrible thirst. Four glasses of water later, I was finally hydrated enough to function.

I had some Silvadene packets left from the time I burned my right leg on an ember at a cook out party four weeks ago. I went to my desk and pulled out the yellow packets. The dream was written on one of the packets!

I sat on my leather couch. On a new packet I wrote down the signs I saw in my mind:

-The water will turn to wormwood and the people will be sickened by it;

-The child will suffer for the sins of the parent because of his inequity;

-The star of the morning will fall from the heavens;

-The temple of Solomon will be rebuilt;

-A star will explode in many places;

-The next a child will lead them.

The last sign: A great darkness will cover the earth.

I dropped my pen and lay on the couch. The rest could be written later. For now, I must rest.

I closed my eyes, and the images replayed on my eye lids, forcing me to look at what I wanted to escape.

I decided to rise and finish writing the dream before the images made me crazy.

Chapter Two

The orange sun hung high in the sky, a dark blue sky with fluffy white clouds. It was beautiful day in a beautiful world.

Ana stepped into the sunlight, shutting out the darkness inside.

Frank, her next door neighbor, gave her a quick wave and she reciprocated. He was a retired fireman with snowy white hair and deep blue eyes.

Ana backed her green Volkswagon out of her driveway, and drove to her office. She would have to stay late that night for taking off the prior day.

Most of her clients were still in school, so most of her patients in the morning were young adults.

One of them, Sara, was waiting at the door. She and Donna were Ana's favorite patients.

"Hi, Ana," Sara said.

"Hi, hon. I am so sorry about yesterday," Ana said.

"It's fine," Sara said.

The two marched up the stairs, joking and laughing as they went.

Ana unlocked the glass door to her office, and led Sara into the main waiting room, flicking on the lights as she went.

The two sat on the large overstuffed chairs, facing each other. Ana turned on her recorder. She always told her patients she was recording them, but would never allow anyone to hear the recording except herself.

Recording her sessions gave her the ability to reassess what was said. Many times there was information she missed, but the recorder reminded her. People generally said more than they realized they were saying.

"How have you been, Sara?" Ana asked.

"Good. I'm focusing on moving forward with my life." she replied.

The session went well, and Ana gave her a quick hug before she left.

Ana believed it to be important to have physical contact with her patients, especially if the issue of touch was a problem for them. With her younger patients she would hold hands. As time went on, it would usually progress to a hug. With physically abused children, it took a long time for productive progression.

Ana understood that her patients would have relationships in which touch would be important: the touch of a boyfriend or spouse, and even the touch of their child. They had to learn the proper ways to touch and be touched.

Ana ran her fingers through her light brown hair, twisted it into a knot, and used a black band to keep it in place.

The rest of the day was a blur to her.

At six-thirty she finished with the last patient: a young eight year old boy named Griffin. His parents were divorced and he was used as a pawn between them. The school mandated he see her. He would draw pictures of his mother on the ground with knives stabbing her and army tanks about to run her over. Needless to say, Griffin had issues to work through with his parents.

The first five sessions with Griffin were with him, alone. After that she alternated with Griffin alone and with Griffin and both parents. The family was making great strides. Griffin learned that the divorce was not his fault or his parents' fault, that they loved him no matter what.

Ana locked the office and headed to Saint Michaels Church. Being a Roman Catholic was very important to Ana. Her faith played a major part in every aspect of her life.

Walking up the cement steps to the rectory, she thought of what she wanted to say when inside so as not to appear totally insane. She pushed the black door bell and heard the ringing inside.

"Hello," a woman's voice responded.

Ana lost her voice for a minute. "Uh, yes, hello," she replied, finally. "Could I see Brother Antonio?"

"Do you have an appointment?" The female voice asked?

"Um, no I don't, but it is very urgent," Ana said.

The next sound she heard was a buzzing.

Quickly figuring it out, that the sound was the unlocking door latch, she opened the heavy brown rectory door and forced herself into the small foyer.

To the right of her was a light brown desk with a very old woman sitting behind it. Her glasses were too large for her petite face.

"Hi, I'm Ana Caine," Ana said, introducing herself. "I'm a parishioner here at Saint Michael's. I really need to speak with Brother Antonio."

The woman smiled. "Come with me, dear, and he'll see you in a few moments," she said. She could not have been more than five feet tall. She was very spry for her age, as she led Ana to an office.

Ana sat down in a chair at one of the two chairs in the room. The room was encased in bookshelves from the ground to the ceiling, except for where the door was located. She already felt better by just being there. If anyone had an answer to her questions, Ana was sure the answer could be found in that room.

The door opened and in came Brother Antonio. Ana rose out of her chair. "Hi, I'm Ana Caine," she said.

"Nine-thirty mass," Brother Antonio replied, recognizing her.

"Every week. I'm one of your Eucharistic Ministers," Ana said. She would usually give a wave to him on her way out.

He was a monk. Most churches did not have monks, and Saint Michaels was blessed to have him. He was on sabbatical after four months in South Africa, working with people affected by a severe drought.

After each mass, Ana wanted to say hi to him, but he was always surrounded by a gaggle of old women, giggling at his every word.

She wasn't sure he ever saw her until this meeting. It was a big parish.

Ana paused, searching for the right words.

"Ana, it's okay to tell me whatever is bothering you," he said.

"Please," she said in a distraught voice. "Please don't think I'm insane, Brother, but I'm not sure where to turn."

Her story came out in a burst of words. At one point she rose, and paced back and forth. Every detail she could remember, she told him. When she finished, she collapsed into the chair, having spent every ounce of energy she had.

She stared at the white ceiling, her head tilted back, relieved to get rid of the information inside her.

Brother Antonio walked out of the room.

He's probably going to get the men in the white coats, Ana mused.

She heard the door re-open, and saw a data stream which he placed in front of her. It read 'Notice from the Papacy.'

Ana sat up straight, taking the data stream from him. As she read, he explained.

"The Pope asked us to watch for parishioners speaking of Revelation, of the Apocalypse, and here you are," he said. Smiling at her softly, he covered her hand with his.

Meantime, to the south, in Kerrville, Texas, Levi James was finishing a set at the Jazz Hole lounge. He was just rehearsing, and it was not a show presentation.

He saw a man at the front table. Something was different about him, he couldn't put his finger on it.

After turning off his electric piano, he walked off the side of the stage. Several steps later, the man stood in front of him.

"Hello," the man said

"Hello," Levi replied.

The man was about six feet tall and exceedingly good looking, dressed in a black pin striped suit. "My name is Peter Ellens," he said. "I can help you with the dreams you've been having."

Levi's eyes widened. He told no one about the dreams. He saw an empty booth and motioned for the man to sit down.

"How do you know about my dreams?" Levi asked.

"We know a great deal about what is happening now, and what will happen in the future. I am part of a secret society known as LORE. It stands for Legion of Religious Elders. It was foretold that you would receive these dreams," Peter said.

Levi wondered if they knew about the girl in his dreams. He decided he would not mention her.

"What exactly am I supposed to do about these dreams?" Levi asked.

Peter put a hand on Levi's outstretched arm and looked deep into Levi's eyes. "Look around you Levi. What do you see happening? Children are killing other children just to see how it feels. Mothers are turning on their children and drowning them in tubs of water. People are turning their backs on God and Christ. The time is at hand for the end to come," Peter said.

"You are talking about millions of people dying," Levi told him. He was horrified by what Peter said.

"Come with me and let me show you what we are talking about. You can leave at any time, but I really think you should see what we stand for," Peter told him.

The two men walked out of the bar together. Peter pointed to his red Porsche.

Levi ran his fingers over the hood, covered in black leather. A huge smile came to his face.
"Nice," he said.

"Yeah, it's one of the perks of belonging to LORE."

The two men got into the car and Peter peeled out, heading for route sixteen and then to 290, straight for Austin.

Back in Michigan, Ana finished reading the Papacy data stream.

"What am I supposed to do?" she asked. "I am one person. How am I supposed to save the world?"

"Do not despair, Ana, for Noah was one person, Moses was also just one person," he said. "It is in the most dire times that God finds someone to be the light. God has chosen you to be a witness, to be a prophet. Let yourself be open to the spirit and don't give up."

"I saw him," Ana said. Looking up at Brother Antonio, the tears streamed down her face. "I saw Christ. I stood before him and he was so beautiful. He gave me a message to give to the people. I felt his grace inside me." Ana brushed back tears as Brother Antonio pulled her up and hugged her tightly.

"Ana, let God's will be done," he said.

She cried uncontrollably on his shoulder. Pent up stress and frustration all came out through her tears.

"Ana, I promise you we will get through this. The church will help you, and there are many volunteers who will come and help us. Come on, let's get some pie. Pie can cure everything," he said with a smile.

They walked out of the brown brick Rectory together.

"I'll drive," Ana said.

"Okay," he replied.

She pulled away in her VW, looking for the closest 'By Buy American Pie' restaurant. She found one, she parked the car, and they entered the restaurant.

She and Brother Antonio enjoyed their fill of apple cream cheese pie and hot coffee. They talked about work, laughing at the everyday problems they had in common. She felt better, knowing she did not carry her burden alone. Placing her hand over Brother Antonio's hand, she said, "Thank you."

"It will be all right, Ana. I promise you." he told her.

Levi took out his cell phone, and called his friend, John. Thankfully, he got the answering machine.

"This is Levi," he said into the phone. "Hey. I'm not gonna make it tonight. Something important came up."

The sun was setting when Levi drove into Austin. His first look at the enormous complex of LORE was amazing. There were four, five-story white brick buildings.

He pulled up to the front of the complex, and a well dressed young man opened the car door.
"Good evening Mr. James," he said.

Levi was taken aback.

"Good evening," he replied, wondering how this person knew his name.

He walked to the massive silver door to the complex. The great door opened before them. Levi had to admit that was cool. He had never seen a door made of pure silver.

Inside, he saw a great hall with a long dining table and wood engraved chairs. It was magnificent, and Levi's mind reeled at seeing such an expansive place. A thousand people could fit in this room easily, he considered.

A tall, well dressed man approached them.

Levi noticed an uncomfortable feeling inside his chest. The closer the man came the greater the feeling. Levi could not bring himself to look at the man.

What am I doing? This is ridiculous, he thought to himself, as the man extended his hand toward

Levi.

Levi didn't want to, but he extended his hand.

As the man's hand clamped down on his, Levi's eyes were drawn upward. Their eyes met, and time slowed down.

Levi's awareness darkened. Everything around him and the man faded away. Swirling air of different colors surrounded them. Blue and green, red and purple colors moved about them like a cyclone.

The colors turned to silver, surrounding the two men, and finally encompassing them.

Levi looked at the man's face, and saw it was beautiful: long black hair with speckles of gray, dark tan skin with the most amazing brown eyes. Levi felt an immediate love for him. A single tear rolled down his cheek. Just then the man let go of his hand.

"I am so pleased to meet you, Levi. My name is Christiant," he said.

Suddenly, Levi's visions returned to the great hall and no one seemed aware of what happened. His right palm was itching. He gently scratched it with his left index finger.

"We are pleased to welcome you to LORE," Christiant said.

Levi held onto the chair next to him to steady himself.

"Let us show you a room where you can freshen up," the man said.

Levi was afraid that if he didn't sit down soon, he would pass out.

Peter took his arm and helped him into a room down the hall. In the room there were two overstuffed chairs, a brick fireplace and a bathroom.

He sat in the first chair he could reach, with Peter's help. He felt a little embarrassed.

"Are you all right?" Peter asked.

Yeah, I'm fine," Levi replied. He rested his head on the brown and green chair, and looked out the window. He was not sure what happened to him, but it seemed like no one else was aware of it, except maybe Christian, who did not react as if anything happened.

Levi felt strong enough to go into the bathroom, and as he walked up to the toilet, the seat raised on it's own.

After using the bathroom, he went to the marble sink and used the gold soap dispenser and air dryer.

His right hand was still itching. He looked at it, and saw a red imprint, as if it was burned into his palm. It looked like a face, or a letter 'T'.

This day could not get any stranger, Levi thought, as he left the luxurious bathroom and headed back to the great hall.

"All right, so, I'm here. Tell me what is going on," Levi said, as Christian entered the room.

Christian was the first to speak. "Levi, our group is the Legion of Religious Elders," he began, "and it has been around since the second century. No one knows of our existence. Our anonymity comes at a high price. We have been tracking the signs of the Apocalypse and have uncovered evidence that you play an important role in what is to come."

"How do you know about me?" Levi asked.

"We have known about you since your birth,"

Peter interjected.

Christian smiled at Peter and continued. "You, Levi, are the seventh child of all boys and you were born on January first, two thousand and ten, the night of a blue moon. You are the great prophet who was foretold to us," he said.

Levi sat stunned. "A prophet. What am I suppose to be doing? I can't save the world," Levi told them.

"Oh, my boy, you are not supposed to save the world. You are suppose to help end it." Peter placed his arm around Levi.

"The end of the world is not a sad thing. Jesus will return and we will have a thousand years of peace," Peter told him.

"But, what about all the destruction? All the lives that will be lost? How is that acceptable?" Levi asked.

Christian was the first to reply. "Look around you, Levi. Between the drug addicts and the euthanasia, the crumbling economy, famine and plagues, theft and murders and more and more people leaving the church, society is crumbling and there is no way it can be saved. This is a new way for the world to start over."

"Please, Levi, stay with us and just see what we are offering you," said Peter.

"I can stay tonight, but I have to be back tomorrow for work. I am a chaplain at a local hospital. However, I didn't bring any clothes," he said.

"We have closets of new clothes. Peter will take you there," Christian said.

Peter led him down a different hall. "Here we are," Peter said, opening a dark stained oak door.

The clothes were on a dry-cleaning rack, and with a push of a button, they moved. The whirring sound of the rack was soft and quiet.

Levi stopped the rack at white male briefs, and picked out his size.

"How about T-shirts?" Peter asked. He found Levi's size, and pulled out a blue T-shirt, then added a pair of blue jeans.

Levi rubbed his hand over the red mark. He turned to Peter and raised his right hand. The mark was on Peter's hand too. Not a red color but a darker brown color.

"What did he do to us?" Levi asked.

"What did he do?" Peter looked shocked by the question. "They didn't do anything to me," he said. "Come with me," he added, leading him into a room at the end of the hall, where he pulled back come curtains to reveal a classroom of people behind a two way mirror.

"Some are as young as ten years old," he said to Levi. "Some are in their sixties. These people are the worst of the worst: murderers, pedophiles, rapists. These people were thought to be a waste of good air. I was one of them, a small time thief who could not find a friend in the world. Then Christian came to see me in prison. Made me an offer of salvation. Now, my business is to care for my fellow man, to await the return of the Lord."

Levi looked through the double mirror. All the people there were working on laptops. Even with nice clothes and good grooming, Levi could tell these were not a normal group of people. One guy was tattooed all over his head, arms and face. A young boy of about twelve raised his right hand to answer a question an instructor asked.

Levi gasped. There it was. The same mark in the middle of his hand.

"What did he do, Peter?" Levi asked.

"He lived with his parents, who were drug addicts. They were both on PNT, what is usually called peanut, in slang."

"I'm so sorry," Levi said. PNT was ten times more addictive than heroine. Its use actually stopped the use of heroine on the streets.

"His father was very abusive. One day he couldn't take it anymore. In a fit of rage, he killed his parents and the other addicts who lived in their house. Then he lit the house on fire. When the authorities sorted through it all, twenty seven people lost their lives. He was placed in a prison for the criminally insane. I was his preceptor when he first came to us. He used to tell me he heard voices, and they told him what to do," Peter said.

"Did you believe him?" Levi asked.

"At that time, I did. The point is, he has found purpose and peace here. I hope you will, too," he replied.

Levi laughed softly.

"I already have peace. Nothing will change that."

"Come on," Peter said, "I'll show you to your room."

The two men went down the hall together.

Back in White Fish Point, Michigan, Ana was on her way home. She was so grateful and blessed to have Brother Antonio as a friend.

A frightening thought kept reoccurring in her brain, the thought that the dreams were really a sign of mental instability. She worked with people who were mentally ill. To say you have strange thoughts is one thing. To say you stood before Jesus Christ is another.

She pulled her car into her garage, and it automatically closed behind her. She stepped into the house, turned on the lights, flipped on the television, and got herself a glass of wine.

After two glasses of Merlot, she was ready for bed. She hoped the wine would make her sleep without dreams, to sleep for nothing more than to rest her mind and body. But that would be too much to ask.

Ana dreamt. In her dream she was flying again, dressed in the white long gown. There were fires in the distance over Toledo and a trail of destruction leading away from the city and towards Cincinnati.

She was following the path of destruction.

When she looked up, she saw the three Angels floating in the air and waiting, waiting, with their swords in their hands. What were they waiting for? She looked around, frantically.

She saw the man with the seven green snakes and bald baboon heads. He was on the ground in front of her. The mouths of crushing teeth were breaking through concrete to get to the tasty morsels of children on the inside.

She looked across at the first angel. He was a massive creature at least twenty feet tall, who wore a gown of immaculate gold.

She had never seen a garment shine that way. It appeared to be glowing. The wings bristled slightly.

Maybe I could try to stop it, she thought.

She kept thinking of all the souls below her. Were the good to be sacrificed with the evil? Was there any city in the United States that would be spared?

She looked at the first angel. Her mind screamed the words, "Stop! Don't do this! Please!" She opened her mouth to speak, but no words came out.

She could not get her body to function, to say what she needed to say.

There came a light of white and blue that looked like someone opened a window and the light shone through. She was at peace in her soul.

The first angel descended into the city of Cincinnati. He was engulfed in a white and orange light as he landed with a thump.

Ana heard the same guttural cries she heard before. She felt a pain in her chest, knowing people were suffering, and that their suffering would get much worse.

She watched the angel, and wondered if he knew what he was doing. She wondered if he had a choice. He was a servant of God. She also wondered if they were the angels of Sodom and Gomorrah. Or, were they the angels in the den with Daniel? Were there different angels for different occasions? Was this the angel that appeared to Mary and the wise men, to Joseph or to Abraham? Were those the angels of light and creation? Were these the angels of death and destruction?

She watched as his great white wings spread open.

Then the angel with burned eyes and golden robes, spread his arms, and a terrible cold descended into the city. The whimpering of the dogs and cats could be heard from all corners of the city. The birds fell like water from the sky and the trees. Many birds fell from the telephone lines where they liked to perch.

Suddenly, she was descending to the city. Unlike the time she was trying to go into the city, she did not feel she was moving of her own accord.

The angel was looming up in front of her. He stood about five feet away. He looked like a statue to her. On the ground in front of him was a Judas tree. It also was frozen and covered in ice.

She wanted to touch the angel. Looking across from her, she saw Levi. She was able to slowly raise her right hand and signal hello.

He slowly raised his right hand. It was then Ana saw something glowing on the inside of his hand. She wondered if the angel burned him, too.

Then she was pulled back, up into the sky overlooking Cincinnati.

The first angel sheathed his sword and disappeared.

She saw seven trumpets in the sky above her.

They cried out a beautiful sound, and the second angel descended into the city.

She did not remember any trumpets in her earlier dreams.

The wings of the second angel were white, and her gown was black silk, with many layers. She, too, brandished a sword. With burned out eyes and white hair, she was striking to look at. She landed on the ground and the darkness spread out from under her feet.

The people came like the thousands before them. Out of their homes, they burst, to escape the death that stalked them. They had blood pouring out of their ears and nose, coursing from their mouths, from their insides. Most bled out instantly, and they became the lower pile on which the other bodies fell.

Ana saw pictures of the Ebola virus. This was ten times worse than any virus that could be heaped upon the human race.

She watched as people tripped on the bodies in front of them and did not have the strength to get up.

She focused on a man in the middle of the street trying to get up.

There was a white flash. He was a tall white man with red hair, and he was suddenly in a bedroom with his son, a little boy with blond hair. He was beating the boy with a leather strap. The boy was maybe five or six years old. He threw him into a mirror and it broke.

He grabbed the kid's arm, and yelled at him for

breaking the mirror. The boy looked like a rag doll. He was dead. Realizing the boy was dead, the man put the body in a large garbage bag, and dropped it into a green metal garbage can outside the house.

Ana was back in the street, watching the man gasp for breath, He was drowning in his own secretions.

Why was she seeing this? It almost appeared like someone was showing her why the judgment should happen.

She saw the second angel sheathe her sword, and disappear in a burst of fire that surrounded her.

Then the third angle came down. His skin was as black as night, with black hair, but with white skin over his eyes as if he wore a mask. His wings were black and magnificent to behold. When the sandals on his feet hit the ground, the ground opened. Hundreds of sparrows flew up from the inside of the Earth. Their chirping was so wonderful.

The third angel opened his arms, and as fire rose from inside him, he spread it out in all directions.

The fire raged, burning the bodies of the dead.

Out of the hole where the sparrows came, lava flowed in every direction, eating up everything it came in contact with.

Ana wanted to cry for the people of Cincinnati, but alas, she had no tears left. She had only the pain in her chest and the burn on her hand from the run-in with the other angel.

Ana had to watch for the signs before the end would come. She had to warn the people. Could they change? Most importantly would they change?

Her heart began to race, for out of the ruins of the city the beast arose. With his six clawed legs, he stepped into the ashes around him. It had the head of a goat and the body of what looked like a tarantula. It also moved like a tarantula. It also had huge sores all over its body. Wherever the pustules would drain, a great fire would erupt.

The name of the beast suddenly came to her. It was Extinction.

She watched as it snacked on the burned bodies not yet consumed by the lava.

The trumpets were sounding again as the creature moved from place to place, ripping off arms and legs as if it had not eaten in a very long time.

She knew that was true, that it hadn't. It made a horrible sound as if it were screaming. I wanted to cover my ears to block out the awful sound.

The huge man with no face and seven green snakes attached to his abdomen stood ready at the south end of the city, waiting for the sign to begin again.

How many cities would fall, either by the Angels' destruction or by stars falling to the Earth the way Los Angeles had gone? This was not symbolism, this was reality, Ana thought. If I can't stop this, my world will be destroyed, she thought.

She looked at Levi.

She suddenly felt herself being pulled back into her body. The lights surrounded her as she was taken back to her bed.

She awoke screaming, lying there, sticky from the sweat. She felt gross. She looked over, but could not see her clock. No matter. The darkness told her it was not yet morning. She would write the dream in the morning before work.

She wondered where Levi was, and if they awoke at the same time. She wondered if he knew more than she did. Did he know how to stop this? She asked herself, for she knew that she did not.

In the compound of the Legion of Religious Elders headquarters, Levi sat straight up in bed, as if he were running from the hounds of hell. A layer of sweat dripped off of him and onto his sheets. He would write down the dream down in the morning.

He had no choice about writing it down. The girl also had a mark on her hand. He wondered how she got it. Maybe the Legion of Religious Elders knew about her, too. So why didn't Peter say anything? He was going to wait this out, release no information about the girl, until he knew more.

His right hand was itching again. He reached over with his left hand and scratched it until it stopped. He closed his eyes, hoping to return to sleep.

When his eyes opened, he was in the middle of a street. It looked like Israel, but not the Israel of today. It was in the days of Solomon, he knew, because he was standing in front of Solomon's temple.

The people were dressed in worn clothes, which protected them from the wind and sand.

Walking towards the temple, he felt drawn to it. Just outside the entrance, he saw a short man covered in a brown robe. His eyes glowed red.

There was another man, much taller, wearing

the same brown robe. He could not see his face but the man with the red glowing eyes gave something to him.

Just then the phone rang. Levi thought at first it was part of the dream, then realized it was real. Rolling over, he picked up the phone

"Hello," he said.

"This is your wake up call. It is now six thirty a.m.," the recorded voice said.

"Thanks," Levi said wondering why he was thanking a recording.

He dragged himself out of bed, and headed for the shower, feeling as if every muscle in his body has been attacked. He wondered if the dreams were going to kill him. No matter, it was a new day and he would deal with whatever struggles he encountered.

Chapter Three

The morning light came too early. "I don't want to get out of bed," Ana said, aloud. It didn't help. I'll shower first, she thought, and get rid of the sweat from the dream.

The water was hot and felt wonderful. She was working conditioner into her hair when it hit her, "The internet! Put the dream online!" All I need to do is go to 'Cell It' where young people went to send in pics or info. It was free to join and everyone loved it. She would type it on her lap top and send it in.

She rinsed her hair and grabbed a towel. She ate her straw bar with coffee while writing down her dream. Always good to multitask, she said to herself.

She was also writing on paper to have a physical copy on hand. But it was much easier to put it online. Thank God for computers.

She sat and downloaded her first dream; the destruction of Detroit. She left out the man with no face just because she didn't want to put too much out there, and if anyone was looking to join her, or if they said they had the same dream, it would be a way to test the validity of what they might say. She then copied and pasted it, and with a push of a button, it was sent.

She took a deep breath. It was as if she were pushing it off her, giving the burden to the whole world to share. She could breathe again.

Her eyes widened. She should have told Brother Antonio. Flipping open her cell, she texted him about what she did.

Her phone rang on her way to the office. At the next light, she read the text. It read: MIT NT B GOOD I D A (Might not be a good idea). The message was from Brother Antonio. She wondered why he would think that. If you have to warn people about something online was the way to do it.

From the moment she got to work to the moment she left, everything seemed crazy.

Jim, a fourteen year old, ran away the night before. She found him sitting at her door. His stepfather was abusive.

She was so disappointed. He and his stepfather came in for family and private therapy, and things had been going so well. When she finally got the whole story out of him that morning, she found out it was a blow up about not taking the garbage out. It was never really about the garbage.

She had a full bath in her office, and she told Jim to clean up while she went to get something for him to eat for breakfast. He was much calmer after he cleaned up, and she returned with breakfast.

He crashed in one of her group rooms, while

she did her two pressing counseling sessions.

Then, after getting Jim's permission, she called his mom and step-dad. They came in at noon on their lunch breaks from work.

Ana ordered out for a deli tray, and with a full stomach, they felt more relaxed. Even though the cost came out of her pocket, she really didn't care.

By twelve-thirty, they were all hugging each other and apologizing. Ana felt a warmth inside.

That was why she chose her profession: to help families come back together. To help people look at the things they do and make sense of their actions.

In many cases, a mother will not realize the biting tone she uses when she speaks to her child. So that child, in turn, picks up on the tone and assigns the message that this is how his mother feels about him.

It was always shocking to see that the people we are closest to, we treat worse than a stranger.

It was seven-thirty when Ana locked her office doors. She wanted to stop and see Brother Antonio, but was just too tired.

When she pulled her car into her driveway, Ana noticed a red car nearby, with two people sitting in it. Probably waiting for someone, she thought.

She ate another deli sandwich for dinner, feeling the dreams were taking a toll on her.

She flipped on her laptop and checked her email. It proudly announced, "You have 2,398 emails, would you like to hear them now?"

Ana stopped in her tracks. With trepidation, she accessed the first ten. And hit play.

"Hi, you don't know me, but my name is Mary. I thought your story was amazing and is it really going to happen? Because I'm thinking of going to college and, well, maybe I will take the year off if the world is going to end. Well, let me know."

Ana responded with one answer. "Yes. It is going to happen!"

Of the first ten messages, seven of them wanted more info or to know if my message was real.

Two were from guys who saw her picture, and wanted a date.

One was scary, though. It was from a guy named Mike Ridem. He felt Ana was sent by Satan to confuse people. He actually threatened her life.

She reported him to the police, and went around the house to check her locks.

She read enough emails for the night, so she closed the blinds, put on her warmest pjs, and went off to sleep.

It would be the last night she slept in her bed. If only she had known what was coming.

Levi spent the day meeting different people. They all talked about how the Leaders of Religious Elders had helped them.

Levi was ready to go home, so Peter brought around his car.

"You ready to go?" Peter asked.

"Yeah, great," Levi said, jumping in the front seat. He was more than ready to go home.

"Wait," Christian hollered. "You have to come see this."

Something in his voice told them it was big. The two men got out of the car and went back in to the great hall.

Christian sat Levi in front of a laptop computer. There it was: the dream he had! Every thought, every movement, every tortured scream. The room was abuzz with people talking about the dream.

Christian scrolled down to the end, and when it stopped, a gasp escaped Levi's lips.

It simply read: "This is the Gospel according to Ana."

Christian clamped down on his shoulder.

Levi looked up at him.

"Who is Ana?" He asked.

Levi could have told him the truth, but something inside told him not to. "I don't know," he said, shaking his head back and forth.

His mind was racing. Why would she put this online? He wondered. There were still nuts in the world, people who would want to hurt you for even saying these things? This information could make her life very difficult. The upside is, he could finally find her. Along with the rest of the world, he added to his thoughts. He scrolled back to her e-mail address. Someone else in the room was faster.

"White Fish Point, Michigan. She is in Michigan," Levi stood and moved over to Peter

"Well, this has been fun, but I have to go to work today. So can you please give me a lift home?"

"Of course," Peter said. "I'll take you now."

Christian waved his hand toward the door. The three were so caught up in reading Ana's gospel that they could not see anything else.

Peter and Levi went back to the car. They talked on the way back to Levi's home in Kerrville, but little of their conversations were about the dream. If the world was ending, no one in Kerrville seemed to be concerned. It was a picturesque place.

Once he was in his flat, Levi went online and found 'Cell It.' He downloaded Ana's address, phone and email. Then he went into Bio Find, and downloaded her name, Ana Caine. Everything was online, including pictures. She was the seventh child like he was. They were both born on the same day: January first two thousand and ten. Her grammar school, high school and colleges were online, her practice in White Fish Point. He even found out what religion she was and where she went to church.

There were pictures of her at different ages. She was strikingly beautiful with long brown hair and dark brown eyes with an olive complexion.

He had seen her in the dreams, but she looked more real in these pictures. It could be an effect of the dreams, but he wasn't sure. He wrote her an email, but thought better of it and didn't send it. The best thing for him, he considered, would be to go to Michigan in the morning.

Levi knew he was about to leave his entire life behind. After notifying his job and the Jazz Hole, he packed up his belongings and put them into storage. He emailed his land lady with a thirty day notice, and automatically paid the next months rent. He packed what he would need, which wasn't much: his laptop, clothes, and cell phone.

He sat on a chair on the veranda of his apartment, and his mind kept going back to the days of Jesus. Jesus walked up to the two men mentioned in the bible, and said, "Come with me," and they did. They were fishermen. They must have had families at home. Families that depended on them to bring home dinner, and a way of life to support them. Yet they rose and did what Jesus asked of them.

When Levi read Ana's blog, he realized he had no choice when he saw the way she signed off the message, 'This is the gospel according to Ana.' There was no doubt. He was being called to the service of the Lord. He was called, and he must answer.

He dropped his key in the land-lady's mail box, got in his car and said goodbye to the life he was leaving.

He headed to Michigan, driving north on Route 35, to White Fish Point and to Ana.

For one night, Ana had no dreams. She slept soundly, and was grateful for it. In the morning, she went out to do errands. She had no patients that day, but went to her office, anyway, to pick up some disks she wanted to go over. She was so wrapped up in the result of putting her dream online, she didn't have another thought in her head.

While driving home from the office, she noticed a lot of traffic, which was unusual for any time of the year. Was it the Parade? No, that was in August? What was going on? She wondered.

She turned onto her street, and the traffic worsened. She felt an ache in her stomach. The closer she got to her house, the more intense the ache stomach grew.

Then she saw them.

News reporters and people she didn't know were camped out on her lawn. Some were holding up signs and looking through her windows. They were like the paparazzi of the old days, but now AMRs, automated with media recording devices.

"Oh my God," she said aloud. "How did they get here so fast?"

She kept driving past her house. There was a girl standing in the street and the cars had to drive around her. She had light brown hair and aqua blue eyes. The sign she held above her head simply read: REPENT.

Ana kept driving until she was out of the area.

Where am I going?" She shouted aloud.

Without knowing how she got there, she found herself at the church. She pulled into a spot by the Rectory, and noticed that the parking area was empty. There was no school in session, and no school meant no kids, only daily masses and Novenas.

She went to the Rectory door, rang the bell, and nervously looked around.

"Hello," a female greeted her from inside.

"Yes, hello," Ana responded. "I need to see Brother Antonio. It's very urgent."

"I'm sorry," the voice said. "He went to the hospital to give last rites. He won't be back until two."

Ana looked at her phone. It was ten after one p.m. "Okay, I'll be back," she said.

She returned to her car. Sitting in it, she felt like the weight of the world was on her shoulders. She needed help, she needed a place to stay. She was tired and hungry. She needed lunch.

She drove to the Denny's, which was the closest restaurant to St. Michaels. She parked and ducked inside.

The hostess in red came up to her. "Internet or no net?" she asked, smiling.

"Net, please," Ana replied.

Sitting in the booth, she could hide behind the laptop provided by the restaurant. Some people wanted to talk to one another, either with the internet or without. She needed a laptop. She left hers at work.

She logged on to her e-mail and it said. "Welcome. You have 11,245 emails."

"Wow," she said, then quickly looked around, hoping no one heard her. No one had.

A waitress in a red and yellow jump suit approached her. "Can I take your order?" She asked.

"Yes, I'll have the smasher Colette with a side of salsa and a cup of coffee," Ana said.

As the woman walked away, Ana started reading her email.

'Ana, I knew the end was at hand. Me and mine are ready. We have gone into our bunker to ride out the storm until the end comes.' Michelle Parker, Salt Lake City, Utah.

Ana pushed the delete button.

After almost forty emails, she was sure the situation was not going to blow over.

She ate her lunch and polished off two cups of coffee. She was finally full. She swiped her card at the table and pressed her thumb against the screen to verify her identification, calculated the tip, and left.

As she walked out the door, she ran into an older woman. "Oh my, God. It's you," the woman said. "Look, Harold. Look who it is," she said.

"Yes, it is really me, but I have to go," Ana told her, while backing out of the entrance, trying to be nice, wondering about the woman's sanity.

She quickly walked to her car. As she backed out of the parking space, she looked in her rear view mirror, and saw that the couple was joined by others. First there were two, then five, then ten, then twenty people.

She quickly drove back to the Rectory, and spent the last twenty minutes parked in the lot. She envisioned herself running through the church and yelling "Sanctuary!" It was not a pleasant thought.

Brother Antonio arrived, and stepped out of his car.

Ana was on him like butter on a corn cob. "Please Help me!" She cried.

The Brother jumped, because he didn't see her approach. When he recognized her, he placed his arm around her shoulders, and they walked up the concrete steps and into the Rectory together.

That was when Ana realized she could never go home again.

A young woman in the city of Detroit was shaking out a small rug on the balcony of her apartment. A strange lightning storm was playing off the black sky. The sun had just set and the lightning was running horizontally all over the sky.

"How beautiful," she said, as she dropped the rug.

The lightning encased her. If only death could have been instantaneous. But alas, it was not.

A strong burning smell dissolved in her nostrils, and then the pain came. It was a pain beyond any she ever felt. Her mind could not conceive what was happening. Time seemed to slow down, and seconds seemed to pass like minutes.

As the burning spread from the middle of her body outward, she became aware of how bad it was.

Then her brain exploded.

The lightning moved down the street, bouncing from structure to structure.

Her five year old daughter, a pretty girl with light brown hair, heard the explosion, and awoke.

"Mama," she said, rubbing her eyes as she came into the living room. Her pink pony pjs shuffled as she walked. "Mama, where are you?" She called.

There was a knock on the door. A male voice called out. "Miss, are you okay?"

The little girl walked to the door. Slowly she reached up and turned the doorknob.

A tall black man came in. Looking at the child, he sunk to his knees in shock. She was emaciated to the point that he could see her cheek bones. Her eyes were swollen and black and blue. Her lip was split. She had old scabbed over cuts on the side of her head. But the worst of all were her hands and arms, which were covered with cigarette burns.

The man opened his arms to her. "You poor baby," he said.

She was leery of him, but after twenty seconds, she went into his arms. When he picked her up she winced in pain.

His first thought was take her out of the apartment. He could call the police. He flipped open his cell phone and dialed 911.

"City of Detroit. What is your emergency?" A voice responded to his call.

"I need an ambulance and the police. I found a child who has been severely beaten."

He was walking from room to room as he talked. Nothing was out of place. As he looked out the kitchen window, he had to do a double take. What in the hell was that? It was burning flesh, like a dog or something.

He moved from the kitchen back to the living room, while the woman on the phone from the 911 service was still talking.

His hand with the phone lowered as he stood in the doorway looking out at the charred burning flesh.

The little girl said only one word, "Mama?"

Back in the rectory of Saint Michaels, Ana was sipping on herbal tea, while Brother Antonio was reading her blog. After reading about half of it, he sat back in his chair.

"Ana, I think you should have come to me before putting this out," he said.

"I needed to get this message out there and this was the fastest way. I have not told you this, but the end is coming soon. I need to be proactive. Otherwise, a lot of people will die," she said.

Brother Antonio came around the desk and sat next to her in the red overstuffed chair. He took her hand in his. Looking deeply into her eyes he said, "I know we have to get this message out, but there could have been a better way to do this."

Ana looked down at the floor as a single tear rolled down her cheek. "What should I do now, Brother?"

"Tonight, you stay here. We have an empty guest room. Tomorrow we will figure out what to do," he said.

"What about my house and all those people?" Ana asked.

"Don't worry. I will call the police and ask them to do crowd control. Get some rest and we will talk in the morning," he said.

He showed Ana to the modest guest room.

She gave him a hug, and he went off to make some calls.

Ana turned on the TV. She loved reruns from the Twenty-Twenty show, even though she thought the movies were weird. Channel surfing, she would stop a few seconds to identify the show and then move on.

She stopped on the news, where a young blond woman talked about a bus accident with a rolling home, an RV. There were few injuries and no fatalities. She turned up the volume.

"Turning to a local story," the newscast continued, "we go to Brett Day outside the house of Ana Caine, a local child psychologist who has predicted the end of the world. No, you are not hearing things. Ms. Caine posted a dream that foretells the world ending. Where, you may ask, does it start, but in Detroit, Michigan. Brett, what can you tell us?"

Brett Day, a male announcer came on. "Well, I am standing outside the home of Ana Caine. Along with hundreds of other people."

He walked through the crowd to speak to some people.

"Miss," he said to a young blond girl. "Why are you here tonight?"

She raised her hands over her head. "I am the way, the truth, and the light. No one comes to the father, except through me." She then wandered off through the crowd.

"Well, I think that says it all. This is Brett Day, reporting." The station went back to an old mummy movie.

Ana turned off her cell and felt she might never turn it on again. This was not the way she was hoping the news would be received. She sat on the bed, and placed her hands together.

"Lord, can't you take this all away?" She prayed. "I know we have problems. There are evil people in the world, but there are many good, kind people. I know, if you gave us a chance we could change things. Also, I do not think I am the best person for this job. Perhaps you should pick someone like Brother Antonio, who is a great spiritual leader like the Holy Father. I am just a plain person who you are sending out to be a prophet. Why would people listen to me? Please do not send me into the belly of a whale. I do not want that to happen. Please, God, give me a sign that I am doing what you want me to do."

She opened her eyes and looked around. There was nothing, just quiet. "You are not good at sending signs, are you?" she said, aloud. "All right, God. I will do what you ask of me. Hopefully, I will be able to make the people of Detroit see how important it is for them to change their ways. In the name of the Father, the Son, and the Holy Spirit, amen."

She lay on the bed and was asleep in a matter of minutes.

She dreamed she was flying again, looking down at White Fish Point. She knew she was covering a great distance, for the towns below her became a blur. Again, she found herself over Detroit. It was different in this dream, though.

She was slowly lowered to the ground. Looking around her, she felt confused. She did not see the angels above her. She did not see Levi. She was alone.

The street smelled like urine, and there was trash everywhere. She slowly walked down the street. She could hear people talking angrily.

A large black man was slapping a young black woman quite viciously. "Don't you hold out on me!" He yelled at her.

"I got nothin'! I got nothin'!" She cried.

He apparently didn't believe her.

Ana couldn't bear to look at them. She started to turn away, but thought better of it. "Leave her alone!" she yelled, moving into the alley.

The man stopped beating the woman. He turned abruptly to look directly at Ana.

Her heart raced as she stepped back a few feet. "Oh my God, he can see me," Ana thought.

He dropped the woman, who fell into a heap on the ground. He moved quickly towards Ana.

She backed out of the alley and put up her fists as if to fight him. Then he walked right past her, looking to the left and the right. Apparently he could hear her but not see her. Defiantly, he stepped into the middle of the street.

Ana pressed her back against the building.

Wildly, the man looked around. He began screaming like a madman.

She was so startled by his actions, she yelped. She quickly covered her mouth, but it was too late to stop the sound from emerging.

He looked right at her. He started moving in her direction, when suddenly a taxi barreled through the street. It hit him and threw him up in the air. His body landed on a parked car across the street from where she stood.

Ana cautiously moved on, hoping the man was still alive.

From behind her, the black woman came. The woman moved past her and pulled out a small knife. She stabbed the still breathing man in the chest. Then she turned out his pockets. She took anything of value that he had. And for good measure, she spit in his face.

Ana watched her walk away until the woman turned the corner and was out of sight.

The man's breathing slowed, and finally stopped. A sphere of light rose from his body. It was mostly dark light, but with a small amount of white light. It came into the center of the street, where it was sucked down into the Earth.

Ana wondered where it went. She looked around. She was alone on the street, wondering what she was supposed to learn from what she saw.

She walked up the street. She did not feel cold or hot. She was very comfortable, which was because, in reality, she was asleep back in her warm bed.

As she walked, she looked at the buildings. One was a grocery store. It was closed, with metal bars across the door and windows.

Every other building was closed and each of them was dilapidated. The only working things in the neighborhood were churches and liquor stores.

Homeless people slept on the side of the buildings; the poverty was so endemic.

Even the rats were homeless. They moved without direction in and out of the street.

The next building Ana saw was a clinic that doubled as a battered women shelter.

Ana knew things had been bad since the depression of 2022, but didn't realize it was so bad.

As she rounded a corner, she found herself in a line. Moving around the line, she came to the front of it to find a young woman with a dark blue van.

The woman was so beautiful, with dark green

eyes. She could not be more than twenty years old, Ana thought. She was handing out packages.

Ana stood close to hear what she was saying.

"Okay," the woman said. "These are sandwiches and soda, blankets and hygiene kits. The Braxton Mission will reopen at six in the morning. You are all welcome to go there to clean up and have breakfast. Our mission offers spiritual care and physical care. Our doctors come in on Monday and Friday. We also help with placement into subsidy housing and group homes."

The people would take the packages and walk away, but the woman was not disheartened by their behavior and kept telling them her message. After the last man left, she let out a great sigh. "Well, God," she said. "I do what I can with what I have."

Ana was so touched by her. "You did a great job," Ana said.

The girl turned around, expecting to see another person, yet she saw none. She walked all the way around the van. Still, she saw no one, so she started packing up the leftovers and closed the van doors. In block black lettering on the side of the van was written 'Braxton Clinic'.

Ana felt a little bad. She wanted to encourage the woman, not make her think she was crazy. Ana followed her as she walked in front of the van, pulling the keys out of her front jean pocket.

She put the key in to unlock the door, when a man dressed in a green army jacket with a gray overgrown beard, came up from behind her. He took his army knife and slit the young girl's throat.

She was able to get one quick scream out, then nothing but gurgling sounds.

Ana cried out, but it was too late.

After cutting her throat, the man grabbed the keys from the lock and threw her to the side of the road like she was a piece of trash. The man opened the door, got in the van, and drove away.

Ana bent over the dead girl's body. "Help!" she yelled. "Help! Please!"

The woman's blood made a puddle around Ana's knees, saturating the white night gown she wore. But, that was the last thing she worried about.

A light rose from the center of the woman's body. Unlike the first light from the man, this light was white, sparkling and radiant, yet it contained a small sliver of darkness.

Ana cried out. The light was so amazing she actually had tears as she looked at it. In the center of the light were crystal structures. There were some things inside the structures, but she could not make them out.

She saw a rip in the street, as if it were a painting with a small piece of the picture torn open just enough for the white light to be let in. She did not see the rip with the dark spirit, but that spirit had been pulled underground.

The tear sealed itself after the light was gone.

Ana stood, drenched in the blood of the dead girl. The bottom front of the gown was red.

She kept walking, and as she walked she would talk to God. "So, if you pollute your soul in life, it is black. When you die, and if you are good in life, then your soul is white. But both of the souls had a little bit of black or a little bit of white. That means no soul is purely good or evil, but a combination of both. You brought me here for a reason." Ana said sternly, "This is what I think, I think that there are good souls in this city and they are worth saving, even if a lot of the souls are bad. So, if that is true, then I have to save the good souls." She continued walking down the street, feeling frustrated.

"Why did this girl die?" She asked herself. "Was she supposed to die, or did she die to show me a message? No, no. Some crackhead needed money for drugs, so he killed her and stole her van."

Ana wished she were back in her bed, or back in the guest room at the rectory, but there was no going back. She had done it now! People would follow her around and take pictures of her to put online. They would go through her garbage and make fun of her on the net.

The modern version of the paparazzi would follow her around like they did the big celebrities of the past.

The worse thing was, if she succeeded in stopping this great judgment and nothing happened to Detroit, then she would be remembered as the crazy lady who was wrong about Armageddon.

Ana was nearly a block away from the van when she looked up to see where she was. She saw a streetlight at the end of the block. She felt compelled to go to it. When she stood under it, the light went off.

There was a house to her right, with old white,

black and gray siding and red metal rails on the porch. The porch light shone brightly, attracting her, so she walked up the steps and opened the heavy, wood front door.

She stepped into a small living room. An old Hispanic man sat on the couch with his head back, making occasional snoring sound. The light of the TV was the only light in the room. Ana stepped through the room, past him, and into the kitchen.

A young woman sat at the table, studying very intently and drinking black coffee. She was in her late teens or early twenties. Her ears perked up a few seconds before Ana heard a baby cry. She dutifully rose from her chair and rushed into the nursery. She picked up the baby and held him close. He was wrapped in a blue snuggly blanket.

"Don't cry, my precious boy," the woman whispered in his ear. Taking him to the changing table, she laid him down and changed his diaper.

A brown rocking chair was her next stop. She breast fed him carefully, with tenderness.

"He is adorable," Ana thought. She opened her mouth and, remembering that they could hear closed it again.

"I promise you, my beautiful Miguel. Your mother will never do drugs again. I will never leave you. I will work every day to be the best mother there ever was. She closed her eyes and hummed while the baby fed.

Ana felt she was supposed to leave. As she stepped back through the living room, she looked at the older Spanish man. He was probably the girl's father. There were pictures on top of the TV. One was of the girl when she was pregnant. The other was of the man and the girl when the two of them were much younger.

Ana crept out of house. Holding the red rails, she walked down the steps, and moved back to the street.

She started walking down the street. "I hope it isn't planned for the girl to die, or the baby or the old man to die. What would that show me?" She asked God.

She kept walking until she felt her body being pulled backward.

She awoke in bed. She felt like someone had physically beaten her. There was a glass of water on her nightstand. She drank the whole glassful, and laid her head back down. It was only five a.m. She had more time to sleep. Thankfully, she was so tired that when her head hit the pillow she was already asleep.

This time she dreamt she was in a garden unlike any garden she had ever seen. There were flowers and dark violet plants with orange tendrils. The grass beneath her feet was as soft as a baby's blanket. Each color was sharp and gorgeous. No one was in the garden. It was bright and warm.

She turned slightly, and saw a cliff behind her. At the bottom of the cliff was a lake with the bluest water. Was it Lake Superior? Ana saw the water of Lake Superior every morning, and to her nothing could look better. It was so bright and warm. She wanted to stay here forever.

She lay on the grass, rubbing her face against the blades of grass. Such peace in her heart she never felt before, except when she saw Jesus.

A sound came from above her. It was a whining sound like a humming bird's wings. Looking up, she saw a pixie made of white light, but the very tips of her wings were black.

Then there were two flying about. The second pixie had black ears. They were playing against the blue sky. The first fairy flew down and landed on Ana's hand.

A flash came over Ana. It was black, total darkness, and was like an x-ray. She saw an image, like a large continent floating in space. On one side was light with a garden holding millions of white fairies. On the other side was darkness with white caves and a house and water. Flying about were millions of dark fairies. The two side views made up the whole.

The flash ended, and she was back in the light.

A thought came to her. It was something she grew up with. Something she heard in religion class when she was a child. "The light of the Lord!" She said in her dream.

She felt herself come back into her body, and she sat up in bed, shaking. This time she was not tired, nor did she feel like she had been beaten up. This time she was at peace.

She quickly rose from the bed, showered, and afterward, selected clothes from the donation box.

The sisters of the church had the clothes washed, dried and hanging on hangers. A job fair was planned for two days later, and that was the reason for the clothes, which worked out well for Ana. Some of the clothes were her own that she had donated.

After dressing, she combed back her Auburn hair, noticing it turned lighter every time she dreamed. She remembered having blond hair when she was three years old. Her mother had no idea where it came from, and she had turned into a brunette by the next year.

After brushing her teeth, she sat down with her cell phone and flipped it open. It read 'your mailbox is full,' in bright red letters with a flashing black X.

Ana read the first two messages. They were death threats. After that, she started deleting any name she did not recognize.

She put down the phone and went to the kitchen, where she was greeted with an eerie silence by all three priests and Brother Antonio.

"Good morning, Ana," two of the priests finally said to her.

"Good morning, Fathers," she said with a smile. Brother Antonio rose to greet her. "Did you sleep well, Ana?" he asked.

"Actually, yes. At least the last couple hours were good," she told him.

"Ana," Father John said. "The Holy Father would like to talk to you."

Ana looked confused. "Are you sending me to Rome?" She asked.

The Fathers laughed.

"No, my dear. A video conference," Father John responded with a smile.

"Oh," Ana said.

"Let us give you a good breakfast first," Brother Antonio said.

It was a feast: big pancakes, bacon, cantaloupe and hot coffee. Ana ate like she had been starving for a week.

After breakfast, they took Ana upstairs to the media room, where Father John brought up the link. "Don't worry, Ana," he said. "This is a secure site."

Ana sat in front of the monitor.

The initial screen read, 'His Holy Father', then a Cardinal appeared.

"Welcome to the Papacy," he said in broken English. "I am Cardinal Basse. His holiness is ready to speak."

Ana shook her head.

Then Pope Thomas was in front of her. The Priests and Brother besides her bowed their heads and said in unison, "Your Holiness."

"Good Morning," the Pope said.

The priests, and Ana, talked with the Pope. She told him everything, even the dreams of the night before.

He had read her blog, but she had not written about the man with no face and the seven green snakes with baboon heads. He actually cried a little bit when she told him about Jesus.

"What was the message Jesus gave you?" the Pope asked?

Ana sat back in the chair. "He told me 'Walk in the light of the Lord and you will never know darkness."

"That is the message, Ana, the message you must get out to the people of Detroit," the Holy Father said. "We will give you anything you need. If for some reason you lose Detroit, do not dwell upon it. Go to the second city or the third city. God is showing you these people for a reason. Watch your dreams closely. The answers may be there. It is never too late for a soul to change."

Making the sign of the cross, the Holy Father bid her farewell.

Brother Antonio took her hand, and he smiled at her. "The Holy Father means it. He has already mobilized the Catholics in the city of Detroit and surrounding churches. We will have an army ready for you."

The older lady came to the door. "I'm sorry to interrupt, Brother, but there is a young man here to see Ana," she said.

The two rose together. "I'll get rid of him," Brother Antonio said.

Ana walked slowly behind him. Peering around the corner, Ana saw the back of the blond haired man.

"Hello, I'm Brother Antonio," the Brother said to the man.

The man turned around.

Ana recognized him. "Levi!" she yelled.

Chapter Four

Ana threw her arms around Levi's neck, hugging him tightly.

He was a little startled at first, but then quickly returned her hug.

"Oh, where are my manners?" Ana said. "Brother Antonio, this is Levi, the Levi from my dreams."

"Nice to meet you," Brother Antonio said, warmly shaking Levi's hand.

"How did you find me?" Ana asked.

"Well, when I looked up your information, initially I went to your house. Which, by the way, you can't go back to. It's a circus, between the crazy people and the media. Then I looked to see what Church you go to. I figured this would be the place to come for help."

"If Levi figured it out, it won't be long until others do the same," Brother Antonio said.

"What about my practice?" she asked. "I need to contact my patients and set them up with another psychologist."

Brother Antonio put an arm protectively around her. "I will take care of everything. I have a friend who owns the Lighthouse. I'm sure you can stay there until we head to Detroit," he said.

Ana laid her head against his shoulder. "Thank you, Brother Antonio," she said. From the moment she put the dream online, her life was changed forever.

Levi and Brother Antonio packed up her house, bringing her only what she needed. God seemed to provide the rest.

On her cell phone she found a message from a friend from school. His name was Thomas Lane. He was a psychologist, and wanted to relocate to White Fish Point.

Ana sold him her practice for a large amount of money. Her house was on the market for four days before it sold.

Levi stayed at the Lighthouse with her after he tied up a few loose ends. He didn't get in touch with the Legion of Religious Elders. He felt ashamed about knowing them, yet he wasn't sure why. He brought his acoustic guitar and electric piano.

There were two small bedrooms, a small kitchen/living room, and one bathroom where they stayed in the Lighthouse.

The two of them took over the maintenance in exchange for free room and board.

The owner of the Lighthouse had his own home. He would come every day to check on the Lighthouse and make sure everything was operating properly. But he was in his late seventies, and coming out everyday was difficult at best. He had spoken with Father John not a week earlier about needing someone to look after the Lighthouse. Put things in God's hands and all will work out on its own.

Realizing it was impossible to find Ana, the crowd that gathered at her house died down.

However, she was still shopping with a blond wig and dark sunglasses. Overall, people are too caught up in the day to day struggles of their own lives to continue worrying about her or her message.

Ana's dreams continued. The destruction went from Detroit to Toledo, all the way to Louisville. Each town fell the same way, and each time the loss of life was overwhelming.

Then the signs started. The first was the woman in Detroit who was killed by lightning and her daughter taken into custody for severe abuse. The daughter was killed in foster care two days later.

"The sins of the parent will be brought down against the child." After reading the article online, Ana needed to clear her head.

She went for a walk without her blond wig, beside the shore of a lake. The sun was starting to make its descent. Sitting on the white sand, she watched the magnificent sunset.

"Hello," a voice said.

Ana turned around to see a young blond woman standing near her.

"Hello," Ana replied.

"My name is Demi," the woman said, holding out her hand.

Ana cautiously remained where she was. "Nice to meet you," she said, not introducing herself.

"I'm from an organization that wishes to help you with your plans," the woman said.

"I don't know what you are talking about," Ana replied.

The woman kept speaking in a soft and gentle tone. "I am from the Legion Of Religious Elders foundation. You should ask Levi about us. We have been preparing for this time, with unlimited resources throughout the world. We could be a great asset to you," she said.

"I'm not sure who you think I am, but you are mistaken," Ana told her, standing.

Ana quickly walked back to the Lighthouse. She was sure of one thing. She did not trust the woman or anything the woman stood for. Her instincts were never wrong, so she never had a reason to doubt them. She didn't look back, even though she could feel the woman's eyes boring through her back.

When Ana was out of her sight, Demi opened her cell phone and pushed a button. "It's me," she said. "Things did not go the way we were hoping... Yes I understand." She closed her cell phone, and returned to her car, a black BMW.

Ana pulled the white metal Lighthouse door closed behind her, and looked for Levi. When she first saw him at the rectory, they had clicked. They finished each others sentences. It seemed they could talk forever about anything. It was an intangible quality, to think he had something to do with LORE.

"Levi," Ana called.

"I'm up here," he said. In the middle of their front room was a white metal winding staircase. It led to the light of the Lighthouse.

Ana walked around and around, up the winding staircase until she was at the top of the stairs.

The great light turned effortless around and around, while Levi checked the controls to make sure everything was operating nominally. His blond hair was parted on the side and pushed back. He had a very pensive look on his face. He was tall and strong. Ana felt she could run away with him in a heartbeat.

But there was more than Ana's heart in question here. "Levi, I ran into a woman who said she knows you," she said.

Levi stopped what he was doing and faced her.

"She said her name was Demi, and she was from an organization called LORE."

Levi came to her side, and quickly pulled her into his arms. He held her tightly against himself. "I am sorry. I'm so sorry I did not tell you," he said.

She backed away from him. "Tell me," Ana said.

He took her hand and they sat on the balcony, looking out at the water. For ten minutes straight, Levi talked and talked, all about LORE and Peter and Christian. Then he showed her his hand, which was something he had tried to hide from her.

She could still see the faint imprint in the palm of his right hand. She ran her hand over the light red mark that remained, unsure of what to make of it.

Their plan was to leave for Detroit in two days, so the remaining time was busy.

Ana called Brother Antonio and filled him on what happened.

He said he would find out as much as he could about LORE.

Ana had been teasing Brother for days, saying that she looked through all of her clothes, and had no sackcloth to wear to Detroit.

After hanging up, she told Levi everything would be all right.

The Catholic Church arranged everything for them in Detroit: Signs, buttons, people to go into the streets with them. Priests, deacons, brothers and anyone they could muster, would be there. They also put through all the paper work. It wasn't like in the days of Jonah where you could just walk into Nineveh and tell the people to repent. A lot of paper work was required in modern times.

A short time later, Ana's cell phone rang. The caller was Brother Antonio.

"Ana," he said. "I spoke with the Holy Father, and they know nothing about LORE. However, his holiness is going to look into it and get back to us."

"Thank you, Brother," Ana said.

She took Levi's hand, and they went downstairs together.

The next morning, Ana and Levi were packing for Detroit. There was a knock on the door. Ana put down the shirt she was folding. She pushed open the short curtains aside on the white entrance door, and she saw a man with a camera. Flashes went off all around him.

Slightly blinded from the flash, she dropped

the curtain and backed away. She could hear the multitude that waited outside the door.

"Ana, can you tell us when the world will end?" She heard. She also heard other questions from different people. Looking upward, she saw the media recording devices. They were held in the air, moving around, trying to get a glimpse of her.

Ana sat back against the bathroom door where the people could not see her, and flipped open her cell phone to call Brother Antonio, who said he was on his way.

She folded her hands together and started to pray. When she opened her eyes, Levi was facing her. He looked to be in such distress that she hugged him tightly.

"We will get through this together," Ana told him.

He leaned in and kissed her softly on her lips.

Ana turned a shade of red, which made Levi smile.

"Oh, don't you laugh at me," Ana said.

"What do you think we should do?" Levi asked. "Shouldn't we tell them everything we know? We have nothing to hide from them."

"The truth be told," Ana said. "I think the media could work for us. It is just that we have to be raked through the mud by them."

There was a knock at the back door, three knocks, then two, then one. It was the code for getting in.

Levi went to the back door and let in Brother Antonio.

"Brother, thank God you are here," Ana said.

The two men laughed at the way Ana said that, which made her smile.

"So, what do you want to do?" the Brother asked.

Ana took Levi's hand in hers. "We need to get the message out. So lets do it," she told them.

The three walked out together to face the crowds.

The girl from LORE was still hanging around.

Ana was sure that was how the press found her. Maybe they thought it would discredit her. Either way, she would turn this into an advantage, by making the press work for her.

The flashing lights were blinding.

"Please, can you stop with the flashes for a moment," Ana said.

The flashes slowed in frequency, and Ana took a few steps forward.

"I have a statement prepared," she said. She pulled out her cell phone and read from its screen.

"My name is Ana Caine. I was an ordinary person until the dreams started. Now I have lost everything. The dreams are more than just dreams. Levi and I have been having the same dreams and we have seen each other in the dream itself. He is from Texas, which tells you a great deal. These dreams are a prophecy. God is telling us that we have to change the way we live. We are not doing the things that God wants us to do, the things that Jesus wants from us. With all our technology and conveniences we have lost our way. Jesus taught us to love God with all our hearts, all our minds and all our souls. And to love our neighbors as ourselves."

She paused. It was so quiet you could hear a pin drop. Hundreds of people stood silently listening.

"Now we are given one last chance," she continued, at length. "We are going to Detroit to try and convince the people to change their ways. We welcome you to join us. If you are unable to come, then please keep us and the people of Detroit in your prayers. You've read my dream as I posted it, and you know what is at stake."

She smiled softly as her light brown hair blew over her eyes. She brushed it away telling them, "Thank you, and God bless you all."

A roar of applause went up as she and Levi returned inside the Lighthouse.

Far inside the crowd a lone man stood, covered from head to toes with tattoos. He did not clap or cheer, but just stood looking menacing toward Ana.

The mark in his right palm was itching. Looking down at the mark, he wondered what it meant. No matter, he had found the true path in life.

Now he was an avenging angel of the Lord. No one would stop the judgment day. He would make sure of it.

Brother Antonio handed Ana a glass of wine. "I have always wondered why the wine in the church tastes so good to me."

"It is a special wine we use, however, the reason it taste so good is because it is consecrated as the blood of Christ," the Brother told her.

"For success in Detroit," Brother Antonio said.

The three clinked their glasses together. After dinner, Brother Antonio left, leaving Ana and Levi to clean up.

"You know, I was afraid to go to sleep at night," she told him.

"Me too," Levi said.

"But now I know no matter how awful it gets, you'll be there with me," Ana told him.

"Are you worried about tomorrow?" Levi asked. "Very worried," she replied.

"What's the worse that could happen?" he asked.

"I don't want to think about it," she replied, as they went off to bed.

Before Levi closed his door he yelled to her, "See you in my dreams."

Ana laughed.

As Levi lay in bed, he rubbed his right hand over the blond hair on his chest and abdomen. Looking at his palm, he realized the rash was gone, but a red imprint was in its place. It looked like a man's eyes and nose, a 'T'.

He wondered what Peter was doing. Peter did not seem to belong to LORE. He thought Peter was out of place there. He was more than happy not to ever see Christian again, and already decided he would stay with Ana forever. They were soul mates, not only by divine intervention, but by instinct. He knew this was where he belonged; at Ana's side, as Ana's husband. Tomorrow would come soon enough. Tonight he needed to rest.

The sun rose magnificently over White Fish

Point.

Ana and Levi had no dreams that night. It was a night of uninterrupted sleep.

When Ana opened her eyes, for an instant, just an instant, she wondered if it had all been a dream. But, after looking about her small room, she knew it was not.

After a quick breakfast, Levi and Ana grabbed their bags. She slowly and cautiously opened the curtain. The mass of people lessened, but there were about twenty people still there.

"Come on," Levi said. "We'll go out the back." He handed Ana her blond wig.

"No more hiding for me," she said, not taking the wig, and heading for the front door.

He followed her.

The people surrounded her outside. "When is it coming?" A young, over weight blond haired woman asked.

"I have children," a young man said. "What will happen to them? Will they be saved? We are good people. We go to church every Sunday."

There were a multitude of questions. Halfway to the car, Ana's path was blocked by a young girl in her twenties. She had brown hair and dark brown beautiful eyes. Ana reached down and touched her belly.

A single tear rolled down the girl's face. She asked, "Will my baby have a life here, or will we all die?"

Ana's eyes softened she spoke directly to her. "If we can change the people of Detroit's hearts and minds, then the world will go on."

Ana walked to the car and Levi jumped in on the passenger side. They drove to Saint Michaels, and picked up Brother Antonio.

After a quick round of hello's, they were off. As they were driving out of the city of White Fish Point, Levi saw a man standing on the side of the road, hitch hiking.

As they drove past, the man starred at Levi. As he was looking at him, the man changed into Christian. Levi pushed his head back against the seat and breathed in quickly.

"Are you okay?" Ana asked.

"Yeah, I'm fine," he replied a little to quickly. The red line on his hand was itching again.

They traveled out of town to interstate seventy five. They were on their way to Detroit to save the world.

Back in Texas, Peter knocked on the dark Mahogany door of Christian's room, but there was no answer.

Christian was returning to his body. He blinked his eyes, recalling that Ana and Levi were off to stop the day of Judgment. There was someone else with them, but he couldn't identify him.

The incessant knocking on the door was annoying him. "Enter," he called out in a gruff voice.

Peter came in a little sheepishly. "Sorry to disturb you, sir. I just got a message from Demi. She was unable to convince Ana to come and see us. Perhaps if I went we would have had a better result."

"You will go, Peter. We all will go to Detroit and make a stand. Round up all of our agents in this area and in the Detroit area. We are going today."

Peter looked at Christian. He felt a twinge of doubt, but quickly brushed it away. Going to the door, he pressed the intercom.

"All personnel are to report to the great room, immediately," he said in a commanding voice. He went to his room to pick up a few things and an overnight bag.

So the Day of Judgment was at hand, and he was ready, Peter said to himself. It would be the second coming of Christ. All his life he sat in Church listening to the pastor telling them to repent their sins because the Day of Judgment was at hand. If that day was coming, then we will be ready.

Peter pulled open a drawer made of dark mahogany wood. His hand was itching where the rash had once been. Christian told him the mark on their hands were how they would be counted. So the Lord would know whom to take.

Returning to the great room, he saw Christian standing at the podium. As the people filed in, he smiled at them warmly.

"The Legion of Religious Elders have one purpose," he said to them. "To allow the end of days to come about. This goal is about to be revealed to us. However, there are those who do not want the Lord to return to us. They will do everything in their power to stop this day from happening. So the question is, will we allow this?" His voice rose. "Let us go to the city of Detroit and the beginning of the end!"

A thunderous roar and applause by the crowd made Peter's heart skip a beat. He walked out with the masses behind, and they boarded the rolling homes.

Rolling homes were enormous vehicles. Fifteen to twenty people could live in them. In the decade of the 2020s, people would sell the houses they could not afford and go in with another family, or relatives and buy a rolling home. Trailer Parks found themselves over whelmed.

By 2024, a new set of parks were created by the government to accommodate all the new rolling homes. After the economy finally straightened out, people bought lots, and kept their rolling homes there.

For traveling, the rolling homes were more than ideal. They were monsters on the interstate. A new lane was made for them because they could do 180 miles per hour.

Peter sat in a black recliner watching TV. He wondered how Levi was doing. He thought about texting him, but Christian had asked him not to. Peter really hoped he would join their side in Detroit.

Christian had been demonizing Ana after he found out she wouldn't stand with them. The only way the earth would be saved was for all people to be judged, he said. Then a new day would come.

Christian would speak at night by the fireplace. He had a devoted group of people who would hang on his every word. He spoke of a thousand years of peace that the Lord would bring. Those who stood by his side would be safe. All they had to do was pledge their undying love for the Lord.

Peter was handed a hot cup of cocoa. There was whip cream with chocolate shavings and a marshmallow stick. He cautiously took a sip to discover it was too hot. There was a storm in the distance. Black clouds ominously hung low in the sky threatening all life around them.

Back on I-75, Ana and company were enjoying the silence. Each wrapped up in their thoughts.

Levi watched the signs for Bay City and Flint, Michigan, knowing they were heading in the right direction.

Brother Antonio was deep in meditation. He had received an email from his Holiness that he had not discussed with Ana and Levi, yet. Back in the days of Fatima, a young girl was given several secrets, whispered to her by the Blessed Mother. His Holiness kept the third secret a mystery, telling the people not to worry.

Now he divulged the secret of the third message. It was that the first city would be lost so that the second could be saved. Brother Antonio wondered how to tell them about this development.

They needed to go to Detroit, try their best, and save as many as they could. Even with the honesty rules of the internet, people did not blindly believe the information they read.

The good Brother breathed in deeply. If he told them they would loose Detroit, it would dampen their spirits. He tried to go deeper into his meditation.

Ana was also struggling with a message. She received two messages from Jesus the Christ. She told no one about the second message. She found herself smiling as the image of Christ ran through her head, leaning in and whispering in her ear.

Ana drove instinctively, her mind off on its own. They were running out of time. She knew they had a day, maybe two, and then they would be out of time.

Ana flipped the news on in her car. They were getting channel 480, the Bay City news. The image of a young red haired girl came up on the windshield. "This is Melanie Gross with the eleven a.m. news. Another Detroit woman was burned to death by a freak electric storm late last night. Her two daughter's bodies were found this morning after a fire started in the neighbor's apartment. The neighbor suffered second and third degree burns over sixty percent of his body."

Ana turned off the show. "The child shall suffer for the sins of the mother," she said.

"What are you saying?" Levi asked.

"It's one of the signs, this one happened already though," Ana said.

"Leave the news on," Brother Antonio said.

Levi flipped the switch on. "...talks with Israel and Iran have concluded and an agreement has been made that the Temple of Solomon will be rebuilt over the temple mount, and worshipers will have equal access to both holy places."

"The temple of Solomon will be rebuilt," Ana said.

"How many other signs are there?" Levi asked.

"Well," Ana said. "A child will lead them, the water will turn to wormwood, and the people will be sickened by it. A star will fall from the heavens and the darkness will cover the Earth," Ana said.

"Let's hope there are no more signs today," Brother said.

Back on route thirty, Peter sat across from Christian, playing a 3D video game. His video game beast was purple with six eyes and four huge arms, and was whomping on a green beast controlled by Christian. He moved his gloved hand, and Peter's purple beast ripped the green one in half.

"Oh, no cheating," Christian said.

"I just hate to lose," Peter replied. "How many people will meet us in Detroit?" He asked.

"Four hundred confirmed, but there may be more," he replied.

"What about Levi?" Peter asked softly.

"I think Levi will have a change in heart after seeing us and our point of view," Christian smiled at Peter.

"Okay" Peter said.

The rolling houses sped down the road at 180 miles per hour. Even though they had their own lane, many were bullys of the highway, cutting in on different cars going much slower.

Peter felt a knot in his stomach. Was it just nerves, or was it something else? While the opposition handed out fliers, they would be handing out cash. At first, he had an issue with that, but after Christian explained it was no more than great advertising, he came to accept it. It is amazing what people will come to accept over time, Peter thought, as he looked out the window.

On the major interstate, the miles per hour for cars was eighty and for rolling homes was one hundred and eighty. No one generally drove the max in the rolling homes, but it would put them in Detroit in one day if they really pushed it.

Peter pushed back a lock of curly brown hair.

"Let's go again," Christian said.

Peter smiled at him.

"Okay. One more time, but no complaining that I'm cheating," Peter said.

In one of the rolling homes behind them, a group of men sat playing cards. All were hardened criminals. All had been tattooed with gang signs, and most were ex drug addicts. PNT was their drug of choice. All were converted to be Christian's army.

"I'll call," a dark haired man said.

"Read 'em and weep," a red haired man said, laying down four aces. He stroked his long, red braided beard, and reached for the money.

The other man pulled out a knife and stabbed him in the back of his right hand so hard the knife went through the table.

The first man screamed, as a blue light ascended from the image on his palm, throughout his body and through the knife to the body of the man who stabbed him. The two were frozen as the blue light burned them inside and out.

The other men moved away in an act of self preservation.

Hearing the commotion, the others come to see what happened.

"What is this?" a young girl of no more than sixteen asked.

John, the head of the rolling home, used a pool cue from the wall and separated the two men.

Moving the burned blackened bodies apart, he caught sight of the second man's palm, which was the most burned area on his whole body.

"What should we do?" The young blond girl asked.

"We'll pull off the road and dump them in the bushes," John said.

They nodded in agreement.

When the rolling home pulled over, the two bodies were dumped behind some weeping willow trees.

"What if someone finds them?" One of the players asked.

John made the sign for them to get back on the road. "It ain't our problem," he said.

Ana was driving like a maniac. She felt it was a time of urgency. She pushed back her light brown hair as she tried to quiet her mind. She had a feeling LORE would not just simply go away.

She looked at Levi, who was surfing the net and watching TV at the same time. He was so cute. She was so glad to have him with her.

Brother Antonio was thumbing through his

bible. It was actually a book. Everything was online, so the need for books was limited. However, Brother Antonio cherished his books. Once Ana walked in to see him, and he was smelling an old worn brown book. She did not miss a beat.

"Do you two want to be alone?" She asked with a grin.

Many times she would tease him about that moment. He stood his ground however, saying that a lot would be lost if we lost our old books.

"Ana," Brother said, as a comment on her driving. "Please don't kill us before we get there."

Ana glanced at the speedometer. It digitally read 125 mph. She slowed down to 100 mph. "Sorry," she said. "I'm a little anxious."

Life was so much easier when she was a kid. Ana thought of her parents and her sisters. No one she loved lived anywhere near the affected cities.

She emailed her mom, who tried to be supportive, but kept asking questions about her practice, her house and her bills. How could she just walk away from it all?

Ana tried to reassure her but was becoming annoyed. When God calls you can't just say, "Sorry, but I can't fit you into my schedule."

Her dad and sisters were more supportive, until the dreams went online. She watched as her Dad was out grocery shopping, and he was mobbed by the media. He tried to be polite, but they asked all kinds of questions about Ana.

Ana watched helplessly on TV as the reporters interviewed her first grade teacher and her soccer coach. One reporter actually asked her sister when Ana's first period was. Ana never meant to bring harm to her family and friends in such a manner.

Thankfully, the reporters stayed away from her patients. Most of her patients were underage, and that made them inaccessible. How quickly a lawsuit would have materialized if they crossed that line.

How many times had she asked God, in prayer, to take this message away from her and give it to someone else? That never happened. She had to accept the mission. She knew that whatever she did, she would follow the will of God.

She entered onto a large green bridge. She pulled the car into the emergency lane, and stopped, opened the door, and stepped onto the walkway of the bridge. The water the bridge crossed was part of Lake Huron. The water, which was normally dark blue, was red.

Levi was already out of the car and quickly joined her.

Brother Antonio was a little slower.

Ana took Levi's hand. "And the water will turn to blood and it will make the people sick and be called wormwood," she said.

"Another sign," Levi said.

"Yes, another sign," she replied.

We have three more to go," Ana told them.

Brother Antonio put his arm around Ana's shoulder, and she leaned her head against him.

"There is so much to do," he said.

They stood transfixed on the bridge, looking at the water, until sirens brought them back to reality.

An officer approached them on the bridge.

"Excuse me. You can't stop your car on the bridge, unless it is some kind of emergency," he said.

Levi was the first to speak. "We are so sorry, officer. Our car was acting up, and Ana walked this way to look at the water."

The policeman stood next to Ana, and peered at the lake. "Oh, my God. The water is red," he said.

The officer called his dispatcher, and reported it, before saying, "You folks need to be on your way."

"Thank you," Ana replied, shaking his hand. When she let go, she made her way back to the car.

The officer held his hand up to Levi so he could see the red mark on his palm. His eyes met the officer's, and a sense of knowledge passed between them.

"How long before we get to Detroit?" Levi asked Ana, when they were back in the car, and moving.

"Two more hours," she replied. She did not trust that cop. It was just a gut reaction. The sooner they got to Detroit, the sooner it would all be over, she thought.

Chapter Five

Peter was taking a siesta. The rooms were small, for the rolling home was an executive model used for corporate outings or meetings. It had twenty small rooms to sleep; a kitchen, a very large rumpus room and three small bathrooms with showers.

Peter's eyes closed, reopened right before he fell asleep, then closed again to let sleep overcome him. His dark curly hair hung loosely around his face. Every muscle relaxed.

When Peter opened his eyes, he found himself on a precipice with white cliffs all about him. He was about two hundred feet up. All about him was space, as if he were on a huge asteroid. Looking down, he was terrified. He felt alone, more alone than he ever felt in his life.

"Hello!" he yelled.

No one answered.

He moved a little closer to the edge. Suddenly, strong hands struck him from behind. He found himself falling, falling, falling. His arms flailed and his mind raced. "This is a dream. You never hit the ground in your dreams. You always wake up right before you hit the ground," he told himself, as his thoughts ran maniacally through his head.

Time slowed, and he was falling in slow motion. He stopped a few inches from the ground. Moving his hands, he touched the ground and lowered the rest of his body to the ground. Lying flat on the ground, his left cheek touched the dirt.

Quickly, he realized his body was cold. Standing up, he rubbed his hands together.

Then the light changed. The surroundings became white, then red. A cliff in front of him glowed a dark red. A small Judas tree burst into flames. The color returned to normal, and the tree was healed.

He did not know that place. There was an acrid smell in the air, and a smell that was somehow familiar.

Then he remembered when his grandfather died. His grandfather's whole right leg was gangrenous. It was green and mostly black. The doctors and the nurses pleaded with him to have his leg amputated. Peter's parents and aunts and uncles pleaded with him.

But Grandpa Joe was not only ornery, he was sure his way was the only way. He told everyone that when he died he would walk into heaven with both legs.

Peter overheard his parents talking the night before his grandpa died. They said he finally relented, and told his nurse he would have the surgery, but before they could arrange the surgery, he passed away.

This place smelled as though a million gangrenous limbs were present. He scrunched up his nose. He covered his mouth and nose with his hand. He had a bitter taste in his mouth.

He moved down a barren road, and his eyes began tearing due to the burning he felt. It was not a place he would like to stay for any length of time.

He looked about him. The wind was very strong, blowing up dust and dirt everywhere. He came to a large pool of water. Moving closer, he could see his reflection in the water. That was when he noticed he wore a long white gown.

The water looked very unusual. It almost looked like it was made of blue building blocks. He had never seen anything like it. The water turned over as if in a block formation.

Peter knelt on one knee to get a better look. His right knee was bitterly cold as it touched the ground. The coldness turned to a burning, like frost bite.

He stood and rubbed his right knee to warm it. Moving closer, he again peeked his head over the side of the pool. The water parted and he saw a face beneath the blue blocked waves. The face was gray and bloated. It was blue around the mouth from lack of oxygen. There was no life inside the eyes of the being.

As he peered intently, the mouth moved, sucking in more of the blue, blocked shaped water. The struggle was brief before the light went out of the being's eyes.

Peter involuntarily jumped when he saw the man breath in the water. He backed away, moving down the road.

He came to an old Victorian house. It was black with white trim.

Peter could only move his hand away from his mouth and nose for a short time. The bitter taste and acrid smell forced him to cover up, so with his eyes watering, he moved past the white picket fence and up the stairs to the black front door of the house. All he knew was that he needed to get inside, somewhere.

He reached with his left hand, and knocked gently on the door. When no response came, he knocked louder and stronger.

Still no response.

Peter could not afford civility at that point. Every second brought more pain.

He turned the black doorknob with his left hand, and his hand iced over, immediately.

He pushed his way through the door. Standing in the foyer, he inserted his left hand in between his thighs to warm it up. But, it seemed to freeze the inside of his thighs.

He assessed the situation. He was in an eighteenth century house. He was standing in a living room with old couches and dark brown end tables. A green crocheted blanket hung over a blue and green flowered chair.

He turned to a see a complete eighteenth century brown dinette set, but no people.

He moved cautiously through the house.

A short white hall led to a kitchen. There he saw a ceramic white table with black and white chairs.

Suddenly, he heard a sound; it was crying, a

multitude of crying, and it sounded like children.

Looking about, he didn't see anyone so he opened the door to the basement stairs.

The crying got louder as he crept down the basement steps. As he came to the last step, he sat on his butt and peered around at the white paneled wall. He expected to see babies. He was surprised to see little fairy creatures.

They were mostly black with small bits of white light. There could have been a thousand of them, but he was unsure. Most were flying about aimlessly.

He saw Christiant, with a large steel shovel, scooping up as many fairies as he could. Turning to the six foot tall furnace, he dumped the fairies into it.

Peter awoke screaming loudly in his small bed. The sweat rolled off him and he was very thirsty. Placing his hand on his forehead, he tried to slow his breathing.

"Just a dream," he said aloud. "Nothing to worry about. Everyone has bad dreams."

He grabbed a bottle of water and polished it off in a few minutes. He would be glad when the day was over.

Ana passed the city limit sign welcoming them to Detroit. She breathed in a sigh of relief. At last they could begin. The knot in her stomach was loosening.

Within minutes, she was in Detroit proper. She moved behind a green rolling home that slowed down while in the city. She got off at exit 216 and turned left at the end of the ramp.

She had seen places in third world countries that looked better than this city. It was hard for her to believe they were in the U.S.

She saw the steeple first. Then, past the row of derelicts and prostitutes, she saw Saint Jerome's Catholic Church. She parked on the side of the church, and got out with her companions, to stretch.

"Let me notify Father Mike that we are here," Brother Antonio said.

They walked to the rectory and climbed up the white stairs. All old Rectories seemed to be built the same way, even down to the white button on the side of the door. Even the sound the little button made when you pushed it was the same.

Ana looked down the street.

There was a multitude of people with signs, begging for money or food, but mostly money.

A larger black man with a red baseball cap was encroaching on another younger man's territory.

The younger man pushed him down, and he fell onto the gutter.

Ana ran over to help him. She did it without thinking. As she helped the man up, he looked at her sternly.

"Give me your money, bitch," he said.

She backed away from him, shaking her head back and forth. She was so shocked she didn't even realize Levi was at her side.

"Come on, Ana," he said. "Some people cannot be saved." He pulled her away.

The older man spit at her, but she was too far

away for it to hit her.

She and Levi walked back up the stairs to the rectory.

"Ana, Levi, this is Father Mike," said Brother Antonio.

A tall black priest with perfect white teeth came to them. His attitude made you want to smile.

"Hi," Ana and Levi said together, which made them laugh. Each shook Father Mike's hand.

"It is so nice to meet you," Ana said. She had already forgotten about the man in the gutter.

"Come and meet everyone," Father Mike said.

They walked through the rectory and into the church. Ana was overcome, for there in the pews sat over a thousand people.

Father Mike led them to the pulpit. "I am happy to introduce you to Ana," he said to the crowd.

The cheering could have awakened the dead.

Ana blushed. The welcome was not what she expected. However, the people were giving their time and energy to help save Detroit.

Ana moved to the microphone.

"Thank you," she said. "You are all God's warriors. The holy Father spoke with me and told me if we can save one city, Armageddon will not come to pass."

The cheers were deafening.

"This will not be easy. Like Sodom and Gomorrah, every soul will count. We have already seen two of the signs, so time is of the essence."

The clapping continued.

Ana turned to Levi. "Let's go," she said.

Everyone went outside with signs they made. They sent texts to everyone within the city. The text told them that they must repent their sins and open their hearts to the Lord. It also warned that the destruction of the city would happen soon, so they must take their families and leave Detroit.

A thousand people gathered in the center of Detroit.

"Split into four groups. Each group will walk north, south, east and west. There is a message you must given them," Ana instructed.

"Walk in the light of the Lord and you will never know darkness. Tell them this message today. You are not just spreading the word, you are saving souls. Let the holy spirit come to life in each of us as we spread this message. If they won't listen to you, tell them their souls will be lost along with their lives," she added, passionately.

The group quickly split up, and went on their way to spread the message.

Ana looked up and saw two media recording devices.

Good, she thought. Her words would be put online for everyone to see.

Levi and Ana, side by side, walked on the sidewalks and in the streets. Their signs simply read, "Repent, for the end of time is at hand."

The first woman Ana saw was welled dressed and in her twenties. She had brown hair and blue eyes. Ana walked right up to her and shook her hand.

"Hi, my name is Ana," she said. "The end of this city is coming soon. You need to repent your sins and ask for God's forgiveness."

The woman smiled at her, "I know you. I read your blog," she said. "So what do you need me to do?"

Ana was a little surprised by the woman's recognition. "Walk in the light of the Lord and you will never know darkness," she responded.

"Okay," the girl replied with enthusiasm, as she set out on her mission.

Everyone clapped and patted the girl's shoulder as she walked by.

"That was easy," Ana said.

Everyone laughed.

There were stores and cafes all down the street and through the next couple blocks.

Ana yelled to them, "Go in the stores and cafes and talk to the people." She pointed to both sides of the streets.

Levi and Ana went into a small cafe that had black round tables with red wooden chairs. The place was filled with mostly middle aged people. Most of the people in that age group were EVFs. They called themselves Environmentalists. The rest of society called them Environmentalist Freaks. There was a small wooden stage at the end of the room, and on top of it sat a boy no more than twelve years old.

Ana and Levi moved closer to him.

The boy had brown curly hair, brown eyes and dimples. When he spoke, the entire crowd was mesmerized by his words.

"My Father in heaven does not want us to go to church on Sunday, praying devoutly for all to see, and then from Monday to Saturday break the commandments he has given us. If you beat your child on Saturday night, it is the height of hypocrisy to sit and pray on Sunday. Jesus Christ is our Lord and Savior and he teaches us that nothing can go to the father unless it is through him. The greatest commandment that Christ taught us is to love God with all your heart, all your soul, all your mind, and to love your neighbor as yourself.

Jesus faced a sadistic and horrible death for us. Who else in your life would die for you? More than that, he did not have to die for us. He could have just as well come down off the cross and destroyed all the people who did those awful things to him. Who else could love you as much as Christ?"

Ana could not believe she was watching a young boy. Some of the best sermons she ever heard would not equal what he was saying. "And a child shall lead them," she said softly.

At that moment the boy caught sight of Ana. "Hello, Ana," he said. "God told me you were coming."

Ana stood silently She smiled at him, and he returned the smile.

Out on the road, the LORE team was busy planning their attack.

Peter watched Christian going over the map of the areas they would hit.

"Our main focus will be to stop the people following Ana. They will be handing out fliers and preaching forgiveness. If you find them, take them out," Christian said. He looked up to see Peter's shocked expression.

"You never told me we would be killing people," Peter said.

"Don't get upset," Christian told him, moving closer to Peter, and placing his arm around Peter's shoulder.

"In any conflict there are those who are sacrificed," Christian said. "If we allow Ana to get everyone in sackcloth and convert them to Christianity, the end will not come. Afterward, we all sing Amazing Grace, and the world will go back to its wicked ways. What we are doing is a cleansing of the Earth. Something that is long over due."

Peter doubtfully shook his head in agreement. He knew the world needed a great change. Hopefully, what they were going to do would improve their world.

Peter wanted to tell Christian about his dream, but for some reason, he decided to keep it to himself.

The rolling homes continued on their way. They were fifty-two miles outside Detroit.

Peter felt anxious inside. He could not kill someone. He stood looking out at the blur of trees as they whizzed by at nearly one hundred and eighty miles per hour. He closed his eyes. In his mind he prayed, "God, please help me do the right thing. Please watch over the people in the rolling homes and the people of Detroit. In Jesus' name I pray. Amen."

He thought for a second, and added. "Look out for Levi, too." He closed his eyes and leaned back against the wall behind him, wondering what the day would bring.

No sooner were his eyes closed, than he was back in his dream. He stood on the cliff facing the opposite direction. Asteroids roared by above him.

He turned all the way around to make sure no one was there to push him.

To the left of him were the white cliffs that turned red, and the burning Judas tree. He could see the lake with the block shaped water. It was large, and there were many weeping willows around it.

To the right of him the cliffs were white and blue. He moved to the right. While looking at the beautiful lake and trees, he was again pushed.

He fell, wildly flailing his arms. He kept saying in his mind, "I won't hit the ground. I won't get hurt."

His falling slowed and he stopped about a foot off the sandy ground beside the lake. Slowly, he lowered himself to the sand. It was soft and warm. He felt as though he were lying on a bed of cotton. He raised his eyes. He could smell the water when the breeze blew through the weeping willows. It was a magnificent scene to behold.

He walked slowly towards the lake. He watched as white swans swam along the far right corner of the lake.

As he went between the trees, the path opened up and a small animal came into view in front of him. It looked like a baby lamb. It seemed to be a couple of months old. It made a high pitched 'baa' sound, and ran off into the trees.

He walked to the water's edge, and leaned over to peer inside the water. It was an amazing crystal blue color, amazingly beautiful.

He touched the water. It felt thick, like pudding.

He started walking. To his right stood a house. It was a duplicate of the other house, an old nineteenth century Victorian. It was black with white trim. He walked through the trees and up to the stairs. Something coerced him to keep moving. He wasn't sure what it was.

At the top of the stairs, he gently touched the white painted door, and it opened. Cautiously, he went through the doorway and into the house. He saw a flowered couch and blue crocheted blanket identical to those of the house he saw in his other dream. And, as in the other house, no one seemed to be around.

He entered the kitchen and saw the same black and white chairs and wood table he saw in the previous house.

As he viewed the white door to the basement, he instinctively touched his left hand. When he opened the door he felt no pain or cold.

He slowly descended the basement stairs. He saw the furnace first and then he saw a man.

The man stood facing him, wearing a white gown like Peter's. His arms were outstretched and a blue light came from his body to feed the furnace.

"Peter," the man said. "You don't belong with him."

Peter, confused by what the man said,

approached him.

Behind the man were more fairies, but they were white with a small amount of black inside them, in contrast to the other ones he saw.

The man touched Peter's shoulder, and in an instant a light flashed inside Peters brain. He saw images of angels and demons and of a great war; demons breathing fire, with great claws and dark purple skin. Angels were attacking them with great swords, cutting off their heads.

Time stopped. Peter saw a great light separating the angels and the demons. The light pushed the demons to one side where they were forced to stay.

The angels flew up and looked at the land. It was barren.

The light changed, and the barren earth became a lush garden, which gave life to the earth and angels to watch over it.

He saw the devastation from wars, plagues and the struggles of man against man. A warrior was raising his weapon, and he saw the shadow behind him.

He saw a demon smiling in the blackness. It was feeding on the rage, the murder and pain, as the acts were committed.

Peter backed away.

He awoke leaning against the metal pole.

Back at the cafe, Levi, Ana and the boy, whose name they discovered was Dante, were leaving.

"We have to go to the center of the city," Dante told them.

The Media Recording Devices were flying about the city. Most news reporters used the old fashioned way of getting the story, with a video cam in hand and a reporter in front of it, but the large newspapers had MRDs. With the MRDs, the news went on line immediately.

"I have an idea," Ana said. She opened her cell phone, and called into it "Everyone meet back in the center of the city."

"What are you thinking?" Levi asked.

She smiled at him, with dark brown eyes sparkling. It was that beautiful smile that won him over. "You will have to wait to find out," she said.

She took his hand in hers, and started back the way they came.

Soon, they were in the center of the city, where there were at least twenty MRDs flying about.

Ana stood behind Dante in the middle of the street. They joined hands, making a star as they stretched themselves outward, with Levi on one side of Dante and Ana on the other.

Dante said loudly, "Let us pray to the Father in the words our Savior gave us. Our Father who art in Heaven..."

Their voices were loud and forceful. Ana was sure this was going directly on line.

When the prayer finished, Ana spoke. "We are all here for one reason. The city of Detroit will be destroyed unless people change. This city will become the example of what will happen to our cities and our world. There are too many murderers, rapists, drug addicts and overall suffering in this city.

If the people of Detroit would come out tonight, sit in sack cloth and repent their ways, then like Nineveh, the city will be spared."

"This is a wake up call that God has given us," Levi said. "And it won't end here."

"This will set off a chain of events that will destroy Detroit and then other cities," Ana added.

Dante moved forward, looking up at the MRDs. In his strongest voice, he said. "Repent and be saved!"

Everyone cheered loudly. They got the message out to billions of people.

Ana warmly hugged Dante. "Great job, Dante," she said.

The traffic was backing up and the people were not so happy about the slow down.

Ana signaled her group to move out of the streets, while waving to the passing cars.

Back in the rolling home, Christian sat in a sleeping room using his phone screen to watch Ana online with Levi and the boy. He tightly gripped the wooden sides of his recliner, and it burst into flames. A low growling sound came from deep within his body. As the chair dissolved in ashes, Christian angrily closed his phone and smashed it into a hundred pieces.

Joe, in the next room, heard the commotion and came to check on Christian.

Christian's face reddened. In his anger and frustration, he grabbed Joe's throat with a hand strong as a claw. With barely any effort, he snapped Joe's neck. Soon the moment passed and he calmed down.

He looked as his phone, and the only thing he said was, "Damn! Now I have to get a new one."

Christian threw Joe's body out the door, into a stretch of birch trees.

Before long, Christian and his group were entering Detroit proper. It was late afternoon, and the images of Ana and her group were all over the internet, and on large bulletin screens on the buildings in Detroit.

LORE needed to make up for lost time. Half of the group was coming in from the west side, while Christiant and his group were coming in from the east.

After assembling them outside of their vehicles, Christiant stood on the cement riser of a loading dock, looking out at the massive amount of people he assembled.

"We are here for one reason; to make sure that Armageddon occurs," he shouted to them.

The group cheered loudly.

We must stop these confused and deluded people who think they are doing God's work. It is God who is bringing judgment to us all. What right do they have to stop that from happening!" He said.

The followers chanted Christiant's name as they walked eastward, to the center of the city.

Peter was the last, like a straggler, but following Christiant as he promised he would.

As they came upon a group of people, Christiant's people went right to work appealing to the crowd's greed. Each person took an arm of one of the crowd's members saying: "If you will denounce God, we will give you five hundred dollars."

Most took the five hundred dollars. Others refused and at that point they were led to the side.

"How about a thousand dollars?" The man with the tattoos all over his body asked a young black girl.

"Not for a million" the girl replied, walking away from him.

Most took the five hundred and headed on their way. At this point, the crowd was dissipating.

Peter came to Christian. "I thought we were denouncing Ana's message, not God," he yelled.

"Peter, calm down. We are giving them a choice. A choice they have had all their lives. This is the choice they made," Christian said.

"That is not true!" Peter retorted. "You're tipping the scales in the opposite direction. I will have no part of this." He stormed off around the corner, and sat against a crumbling building.

Across the street in an alley, a group of three disheveled homeless men stood around a green trashcan. They were cooking hotdogs on sticks. They looked like they had no possessions in the world.

Peter was given five hundred dollars to distribute. He pulled the money from his pocket and headed across the street.

Ana and her group were entering the area as the crowd diminished. Brother Antonio caught sight of Christian.

Christian's eyes sparkled as he saw Brother Antonio.

"Go back, everyone go back," Brother Antonio yelled to his group. Alas, it was too late.

Christiant placed his left hand over the inside of his right hand, over the image of the face T and yelled out. "Suscitatio, damno animus," *(Awaken, damned souls)*.

The image inside every one's hand glowed a painful red. Every one of Christiant's people cried out in pain.

Across town, Levi cried out, grasping his right hand as his eyes glowed red. Looking up at Ana, he screamed and attacked her. Pinning her down on the ground, he wrapped his hands around her throat.

She fought with every ounce of strength she had. Looking into his red glowing eyes she cried out, "Levi!"

He pulled his hands away from her as she screamed in agony. Tears streamed down his face. He rose and ran down the street.

Ana felt many hands pulling her up. They sat her on a chair, stroked her hair and brushed away the tears on her face, some of which were not hers.

Across town, Peter was handing the money to the homeless men. They offered him a hot dog and a stick, which he kindly refused.

Suddenly his hand was burning. Instinctively, he grabbed onto it. His eyes glowed a bright red. He wanted to kill, to rape, to bring suffering to all. It was overwhelming, like nothing he ever felt before.

Then in that instant, the images from his dreams came crashing back and Christiant's words were with them: "We give them a choice,"

Peter looked up to see the homeless men backing away in fear.

Peter thrust his right hand into the fire. The pain was excruciating. He cried out loudly and fell to his knees. His hand was badly burned. Looking up, he saw images of men coming and going. "Please help me," he asked of them.

The first man took his wallet, the second his watch and gold cross his mother gave him.

Peter had no strength to resist.

The third man rustled through Peter's pockets until he found a cell phone. Instead of putting the phone in his own pocket and running away, he called for help. He pulled Peter out of the alley, and stayed next him. He used the water Peter had on his belt loop to wash out the burn. "It's okay," he said.

Peter rested his head against the man's shoulder. He was so tired, even words could not escape his lips.

After the screaming, Christiant's people went crazy, attacking Ana's group. They ripped out hair, broke necks, arms and legs. One man bit off the face of a woman, leaving her to die with blood spurting every where. The acts were more than violence. They were uncontrollable rages.

Christiant went through the crowd until he came face to face with Brother Antonio. Although no one but Christiant could see it, Brother Antonio transformed into an angel with white wings and a breastplate of iron.

At the same time, Christiant transformed into a black and purple demon with claws, yellow eyes and a long black tail.

The two shot straight up into the air, grappling with each other. Christian bit into Antonio's shoulder. Antonio punched Christiant's head as hard as he could.

Meanwhile, flight 1143 from Chicago to Detroit was making its final approach. A small boy of five was looking out the window. "Maa...Maa. There's an angel and a devil fighting outside the plane," he said.

Looking outside, she saw nothing. "I think you're eating too much sugar. No more sugar for you today," she said.

"Oh, mom, why?" he cried.

Back in the city, the followers of Ana were all but dead. Yet the frenzied killing spree continued.

It was not enough for Christian's followers that Ana's people were nearly dead. They also cut off fingers and pulled out eyes. One man was urinating on the dead bodies. Some wandered off in search of more people to kill.

Levi ended up in a dress store. He found a chair in the back, and sat down, struggling to hold back this insanity. He loved Ana. He would never hurt Ana, yet he tried to kill her.

Looking at the red mark on his hand, he saw the image separate and move itself around from T to finally ending in 666. He sat on the chair, growling loudly.

Ana and the others saw the chaos in the street. Grabbing hold of Dante's hand, she screamed.

"Everyone! Retreat!"

She ran to the closest high end hotel and put her credit card on the desk. She had at least twenty people with her.

"Five state rooms please," she said to the automatic registration machine.

"Break into groups of four," Ana told those with her, handing out the electronic keys the machine dispensed.

They went upstairs.

Ana shared a room with Dante and a girl named Marie. She instructed Marie to get in touch with Dante's family, so that they would know he was unharmed.

When Ana knew everyone was safe, she returned to the street to find Levi.

She moved in and out of the crowds, but couldn't find him. She couldn't find Brother Antonio, either. She had to fight off a couple of people during her search.

Running in and out of the cafes through the center of Detroit, she couldn't believe how much it resembled a war zone.

She took a side street around the bodies on the West side.

As she ran past a side street, she saw an ambulance. One of the paramedics lay on the street with a knife sticking out of his right eye. He was dead.

The other paramedic, the ambulance driver, was grappling with a crazy guy.

Ana crept over to the ambulance. She picked

up a metal oxygen tank, and hit the crazy guy in the head.

"Thank you lady, he was gonna kill me," the paramedic said, as he stood and hugged Ana.

Peter ran around the corner, and approached them. He saw Ana.

"Thank God you're all right," Peter said.

"I have to go," Ana said.

"You're trying to find Levi," Peter told her.

"How did you know that?" she asked.

"I know a lot. You need to take me with you," he said.

He extended his left hand. "My name is Peter and I can help you find Levi," he said.

The ambulance driver interrupted them. "I just got a call back to the station. All hell is breaking loose in the city," he said. "I will leave you with dressings saline and Silvadene cream for your hand. But I really have to go," he said.

Ana took the supplies. "Can you drop us at the Marriott hotel?" she asked.

"Sure," he said. "Jump in."

"Wait," Peter yelled. "This homeless man helped me."

They turned around to see no one there.

"He was right here just a minute ago," Peter said.

"We have to go," Ana said. "We will have to look for Levi in the morning." She had a gut feeling that Levi was okay.

Ana helped the driver pick up his dead friend, and they piled in on the front seat.

Unfortunately, the ambulance ran into a group of insane people who started hitting the windows and trying to rock the ambulance.

The driver kept going, hitting one person after another, anyone in the way. "What the hell is going on here?" He cried out.

"After you drop us at the hotel, get your family and leave Detroit," Ana said.

When they arrived at the Marriott, Ana helped Peter inside.

The front desk clerk, who normally monitored the automatic registration machine, locked the doors behind them. "You would not believe what is going on here," he said.

"Actually, I would," Ana replied, as she led Peter up to the room.

Dante was playing video games. He ignored Ana as she came into the room and sat Peter on the other bed.

Opening the saline packets, she cleaned the wound and then placed the saline 4x4s on his hand. What she did would pull the heat out of the burn.

After about three of those packs, she put Silvadene on the burn, with gauze and Kerlix wrap.

Marie brought her purse over. "I have pain pills for my back," she said handing him a pill.

"Thank you," Peter said, breaking the pill in half.

Ana got Peter to lay back on the bed. Taking off his shoes she sat beside him with her knees folded under her. "Marie will call room service and get us all dinner," she said.

Marie nodded her head in agreement.

Ana and Peter talked about Christiant and LORE. He explained about the mark on their hands and how Levi must have felt.

After the burgers arrived, the four of them ate.

Peter's eyes grew heavy and he fell asleep.

Dante soon followed. Ana moved him onto a cot in the room. She and Marie would share the other bed.

Ana walked out onto the balcony. The police were everywhere, hauling away dead bodies and crazy people. She looked as far as she could, and saw the same thing. Tears rolled down her face.

"Where are you, Levi?" Ana said into the night. There was no reply.

Chapter Six

Up in the clouds, Antonio and Christian were battling for their lives. Locked in combat for hours, the effort was taking its toll on both combatants.

Antonio received cuts on his face as the devil's black tail whipped about, trying to do the most damage. The poor man lost a great deal of blood.

Christian was bruised and beaten. His energy was greatly depleted. Then the tail made its final thrust into Antonio's left rib cage.

Antonio's heart was pierced by the ribbed tail. It killed him instantly. He fell from the heavens and landed in the middle of the city. His angelic appearance returned to human.

The impact crushed the street beneath him. He was beaten and stabbed in the heart. He would appear as one of the many people killed that day.

Levi went into the woman's dressing room in the back of the store. There was a small area next to the last stall. Levi sat down and pulled his knees up to his chest. The store closed and Levi stretched out. He was soon asleep.

When Ana's eyes opened, she stood in a white gown surrounded by nothing. Just darkness. No light or sound penetrated the darkness. Just emptiness.

She moved her hands in front of her to see if there was anything there. She frantically groped around for anything physical she could touch: a light switch, a chair, anything. She found nothing. She never felt so alone.

"Help me," she said as quietly as a mouse. "Help me," she said a little louder. Then in the distance, she saw a light. It was moving towards her.

She reached out to touch the light. She wanted the light. She needed the light. She felt as if she would die without the light. Soon, it was close enough to see.

"Brother Antonio," she said softly, recognizing the form inside the light.

He hugged her closely, whispering in her ear. "Walk in the light of the Lord," he said. "You must instruct your people to leave Detroit by the time the sun sets on the new day. You and Levi must witness its destruction. It is part of your purpose in this."

"What about the people of Detroit?" She asked. "Give them the message. They will either heed it, or stay and be destroyed."

"I have to find Levi, he..."

Brother Antonio moved back from her. "Do not worry about Levi. He will come to you," he said. "Peace of the Lord be with you always."

His wings spread, and Ana saw him for what he truly was: an angel of the Lord.

Then she realized there was something else in

the dark. There was something alive, scratching at her.

"Help me!" Ana yelled. "Help me!" She sat up screaming in her bed as the nails ripped into the flesh on her right calf.

It was Marie, who grabbed her hand. "Ana, are you all right?" She asked.

"Yes," Ana whispered, relaxing. "I need water, please."

Dante and Peter were still asleep.

Ana lied back down, but didn't want to go back to sleep.

The entire day had been taxing. She required more sleep than she got, so she did fall asleep.

This time her sleep was undisturbed.

Peter, on the other hand, was not so lucky. He found himself on the cliff. This time he was not alone. Levi stood next to him, staring into space.

Peter touched his arm, and Levi faced him.

Levi put his right palm up, and Peter could see the numbers 666.

"You did this to me. Why?" Levi asked in anger.

"I didn't know," Peter said. He showed Levi his bandaged hand.

A great wind rose and blew Levi to the edge of the cliff.

Peter grabbed his arm with his right hand, screaming in pain.

Levi fell.

Without hesitation, Peter jumped after him. They were on the wrong side, the left side of the cliffs.

Just before the bottom, Peter stopped and slowly let himself all the way down. The smell hit him first. Using his bandaged hand, he instinctively covered his nose and mouth.

Levi stood, dazed. Finally, the smell registered. Making a terrible face, he covered his nose and mouth with his left arm. "What is that smell?" He asked?

"It's death," Peter replied. "We need to make it to the house."

Peter dragged Levi past a burning Lazarus bush, and then past the blocked water with the face drowning in it over and over.

Peter wondered who the man was in the water, and what had he done.

They reached the eighteenth century house. Inside, they sat on the floor just inside the room.

"I didn't know. If I had known, I never would have brought you to LORE," Peter told Levi. "Please forgive me."

"I forgive you," Levi said. "Now, tell me what happened to your hand."

"I stuck my hand in an open fire and burned off the image," Peter said.

"That's what I need to do then," Levi said.

Peter looked around the house; it remained unchanged. "We have to get out of here," he said urgently.

"No, wait, I hear something," Levi said.

"Listen to me. We have to get out of here. Now!"

Peter pulled at his arm as he walked toward the

basement door. "It's black fairies. He is burning black fairies. He burns them in a furnace," Peter said.

"Who is burning black fairies?" Levi asked.

"Christiant. He is burning what looks like black fairies. They have a little bit of white in them. I don't know what they are, but it sickens me to see him do it. Tell me where you are, so Ana and I can come get you when we finish this dream," Peter told him.

"You're with Ana?" Levi asked.

"Yes, now tell me where you are," Peter said fervently.

"I'm in the Boccaccio Lady store on Woodward and West Columbia."

"Great, I will come and find you, wait, wait..."

Peter awoke with his hand out. It was four thirty in the morning and his hand was aching. He took the other half of the pain pill Marie had given him.

Peter quickly put on his shoes, combed his hair, and left, quietly closing the door.

The streets were finally empty. The MRDs had all the evidence, so the police had to match the crime with the person who committed it.

Peter moved stealthily through the streets. There was no guarantee the police caught all of Christiant's people.

He turned right on West Columbia, and found the right shop. He knocked on the window a few times, until Levi finally heard the noise. When Levi came to the window, Peter was shocked at how haggard Levi appeared.

"Go to the back of the store," Peter said.

The front and back of the store had security

systems. When Levi opened the door, an alarm went off.

Peter turned him towards the camera. "Show them your hands," Peter said. They both showed the camera they had nothing.

"My friend fell asleep in the store. Please be assured we are not stealing anything," Peter said apologetically.

"Do you think they'll arrest me?" Levi asked, when they left the store.

"After the troubles they had tonight, I highly doubt it," Peter said, reassuring, him half dragging him through the streets as they made the way back to the hotel.

They found the hotel door locked.

They rapped gently on the door, and the desk clerk responded. Recognizing Peter, he let the two men in. "Is it safe out there yet?" he asked.

"The streets are empty, but I would still lock the door," Peter replied.

Peter sat Levi at the reservation desk. He went to the hotel's ATM, ran his card through, and put his finger on the side for the machine to check the print. He withdrew two thousand dollars. He put half of the money away and faced the clerk.

"You have access to get into every area. I will give you one thousand dollars to let us into the kitchen," Peter said.

The man hesitated, so Peter continued. "Also, you will be saving a man's life, but more than that, you will be saving his soul."

Looking from Peter to Levi, the man finally

consented. "Okay," he said.

Peter quickly led Levi and helped into the kitchen.

"We need a few moments," Peter said, to the clerk.

Peter switched on the stove. The blue light burned. "Are you ready?" he asked Levi.

"Just do it," Levi demanded.

Peter stuck Levi's right palm into the fire.

Levi screamed and instinctively tried to pull his hand away. The screaming was horrible.

Peter fought with him, using his good left hand, and after the right amount of time, he pulled Levi's hand out of the fire. He turned the hand over.

The palm was black and swelling, but the numbers were gone.

Peter rushed him to the sink and put the coldest water he could on it. "We have medicine upstairs," he said.

Levi was mostly moaning.

After running cold water on Levi's hand for five minutes, Peter dragged Levi upstairs. It was five thirty five.

After putting on the Silvadene cream and saline wrap, Peter gave him half a pain pill that he pulled out of Marie's bag. He would tell her in the morning when she woke up.

He put Levi in his bed and pulled off his shoes.

Everyone was still sound asleep, tired from their ordeal.

Soon, Peter and Levi were asleep, too.

Christiant was asleep in his rolling home. Most of his people had been arrested, but that didn't concern him. Ten of his high priced lawyers were getting them out. His followers who worked in the police department kept them all together and calmed down by using an aerosol Xanax.

The police were higher functioning then the group he set loose on the city. Either way, they would all suffer the same fate.

It was morning when Ana and her friends awoke. She was starving, so the first order was to get room service.

Ana was thankful Levi had not been hurt.

"I'm so sorry Ana," he said. "I didn't know this was going to happen. You know I would never hurt you. It was LORE and Christian," he added, hugging her tightly.

"You did not hurt me," Ana said. "When it came down to that, you ran away. Anyway, we need to evacuate the city today. At sundown the city of Detroit will be destroyed. Marie, I want you to gather our people and take them to Toledo, Ohio. That is the next city to be destroyed. Before you all leave, we need to email everyone in the city and tell them to leave. Anyone of our people still alive can hand out fliers. No matter what, by four p.m. I want everyone out of the city. No exceptions, do you understand?"

"What about the three of you?" Marie asked.

"Peter will have to go with you," she said. "Levi and I need to be here. We are the two witnesses alluded to in the book of Revelation."

Ana looked at Levi and he came next to her and held her hand.

"I want to stay with you," Peter said. "I am involved in this and now. I know we must work together."

Ana shook her head. "Anyone here after sundown will be destroyed," she said.

She studied the two men with their hands bandaged. "I guess I will be doing the messaging today." She smiled at them slyly.

The three laughed.

After breakfast, Peter and Levi went off to print more fliers, while Ana emailed the mayor and state legislators. She went online with a new blog for her site. It simply stated, 'The City of Detroit will be destroyed at sundown!'

It took only seconds for it to be picked up world wide. When the guys returned with the fliers, she was ready to go.

Ana left the room and gathered her people. She looked at what was left of them. They went from a throng a thousand strong to maybe four hundred.

Breaking into groups, they headed out on foot in the four directions of the city. Their plan was to pick up any survivors they missed, and get as many people out as they could.

As they said their good-byes, Ana hugged Dante tightly. "Take good care of him, Marie," She said.

Half a block down the real reporters showed up. The questions flooded her:

"Ana, why is Detroit going to be destroyed?"

"Ana, is it true there will be a massacre?"

"Do you expect people to sit in sackcloth,"

Between the light and the cameras, Ana was feeling a little overwhelmed, so she pushed a camera away from her.

She stopped walking. She raised up both hands at the crowd, and waited for everyone to be quiet.

Finally the noise died down.

Ana spoke to them. "The time for sitting in sackcloth is over. At sundown tonight, the city will be destroyed. Everyone in the sound of my voice needs to evacuate. Even if you don't believe what I am telling you! Is it worth the risk of your children's lives to ignore this message? Leave Detroit, but know that wherever you go, this will follow. The truth is, you need to go find your faith in God, but do it quickly. I do have a message for you and this is it: "Walk in the light of the Lord and you will never know darkness. Trust me, without God there is no light."

Ana and Levi walked past the reporters and down the street handing out fliers, encouraging people to leave the city.

Lourdes Sanchez was drying clothes after she put her baby down. She was a Detroit native since she was three years old, and had four children who were all home schooled.

A knock on her door made her jump. No one came to see her. After her husband had died, she really didn't talk to many people. Opening the door she saw two tall men in her doorway. They were dressed in expensive suits, and wore sunglasses.

"Hello," Lourdes said.

"Hello," one man replied.

"Would you like to come in?" she asked politely.

"Yes please, we are very thirsty," the other man said.

Sitting at the kitchen table, Lourdes brought them some iced tea.

Leaning in, the darker man said, "Lourdes, you need to leave the city."

"And go where? With what?" she asked.

"Your husband was a smart man. If you look under the floor board in your bedroom by the vent on the floor, you will find a metal case. There is money there. Take it and leave the city of Detroit. You must leave before sundown, and no matter what do not look back."

Lourdes turned around to grab a plate of cookies, and when she looked back, the men were gone.

Lourdes went to her bedroom. As she walked in, the wooden floor board by the vent was shining like it was made out of gold. She pulled up the wooden floor board to find a long slender metal box, just as the men told her. To her amazement, there was thousands of dollars inside. It was enough for them to start over. "Okay," she said. "Everybody pack!"

Ana stopped at a hot dog stand. She had not eaten a hot dog in years. "Chili cheese dog with everything," she told the obese man running the stand.

The vender began fixing the hot dog.

"Oh, and a large Pepsi," Ana added.

Levi was in the street handing out fliers to passing cars. He already ate while she passed out fliers.

Taking her chili cheese dog and soda, she sat at the picnic table across the street. She wolfed down her food as fast as she could. She daintily wiped the sides of her mouth as if she were high society, and hoped Levi didn't see the way she ate.

Levi came over to her. "Could you get me a water?" He asked.

"Sure," Ana said. She returned to the hot dog vender and bought a bottle of water for Levi.

It was three o'clock and the traffic was heavy as people rushed to get out of the city and work.

Ana checked her blog, and discovered the news reporters, and gawkers, were positioned just outside the city limits, waiting for the end.

"Levi," she said, handing him the bottle of water. "What if the city is not destroyed? They will put me in jail, or something worse. Now I know how Jonah felt."

"The dreams have never been wrong," Levi said. "Do you know where we are supposed to be?" he added.

Ana pointed to the large, blue sky scraper. "The top floor is where we are to be," she said.

"How do you know for sure?" Levi asked.

Ana gave him the look that all women have and can show and all men suffer through.

"Sorry," Levi said.

It was four o'clock. Levi and Ana were handing out fliers, slowly working their way back to the center of the city.

Most of the people said thank you.

A few called them nuts.

One man threw his coffee on Ana. Thank God it was cold, she thought, or they would be sharing the Silvadene cream.

Ana ran into a store and bought a new blouse. It was a longer white blouse, not exactly her style, but it would work.

At four thirty, most of the traffic died down.

"We have to go," Levi said.

Ana was warning people as they walked down the street, handing them fliers. By then her tone changed. She was begging people to leave the city.

Levi saw at least eight MRDs flying about overhead. The sun was starting to set, so he went to Ana and pulled her away from the cars, where she also handed out fliers.

"We must go now," he said, pointing to the sun.

She relented, and the two went to the big blue sky scraper. The store's security guard took no notice of them as they walked through the doors.

They rode the elevator in silence. They had not even pushed a button, and yet the elevator took them to the penthouse floor.

When they stepped out of the elevator, they stood in the most beautiful penthouse home they ever saw. The view it provided of the city was spectacular. They could see the entire city.

On the outskirts of the city were rows of lights. The news teams were ready to go. A few dared to be in the city, but most were beyond the city limits. Many MRDs floated over the city, controlled by the news teams.

They watched as the sun slowly set. The sky turned orange and blue. It was a magnificent view.

God has much better colors to work with then we have, Ana thought to herself. I did what I could, she added to her thoughts.

The sun set completely. There was darkness over the land until the moon rose.

Ana took Levi's hand in hers.

On the outskirts of town the reporters watched the city.

Everyone held their breaths, but nothing happened. Everyone laughed. The girl with the message of destruction was crazy, getting everyone worked up for nothing, they joked.

Ana saw it first, sensed it first. A huge angel, an image of orange and white, wielding a great sword, descended on the city. It was twenty feet tall with golden robes, white hair, and white wings opened wide.

Ana moved closer to the window.

The eyes of the image were burned out. The ground shook beneath its brown sandal shod feet.

When the feet of the image struck the ground, she heard the wailing of women.

Even high up, where she and Levi stood, the sound was unmistakable. It was a cry that comes from deep within a woman's body when she is losing her child.

Ana looked at the reporters on the outskirts of town. Most were running away. Some, without thinking, stepped inside the edge of the city limits.

She found a telescope in the room, and watched close up as a blue light surrounded those people.

They turned into white rock, right before her eyes. It looked like white rock or cement. They were frozen in whatever position they were in when the light touched them.

The MRDs appeared to be operating, but Ana could not tell for sure.

The great angel spread his arms, and a cold descended from the heavens. Birds fell from the trees. The dogs and cats were suffering. No human or beast survived.

The great angel sheathed his sword. The flames encircled him, and in an instant he was gone.

"What good will come of this?" Levi asked softly.

"We will soon see," Ana replied.

They saw a figure robed in layers of long black silk, appear from the heavens. It was a female, at least twenty feet tall, and had eyes burned out just as the first. Her hair was white and longer than the first angel's. She landed close to where the other angel had been, opened her arms, and a blackness rose from beneath her brown sandals. It traveled into the city.

The wailing turned to cries and moans. The condemned poured from inside their homes. Blood poured out from every orifice on their bodies. They fell on top of one another. They were flailing about, fighting for life when death was inevitable.

The streets of Detroit became an open grave. Almost a million people lay bleeding and dying.

Hot tears ran down Ana's cheeks. She brushed them away "Do you think the children were evil?" she asked.

"No, I don't, but I think God had to get our attention," Levi replied.

"He has the world's attention now." she said, hoping the images were online by then.

They looked across the city, at the total annihilation. There was an agonal breath here or there, but nothing more.

The second angel sheathed her sword, and the fire came, encompassing her, and she was swept away.

Ana wiped away her tears as the third angel came.

There was no life in the city anymore.

Another angel, the same size as the others, with black skin and wings, came. He wore a sparkling white gown, with white around his eyes as if he had on a mask. He was a great sight to behold. With his wings spread, he landed on the ground.

When his feet hit the ground, the ground cracked open.

Hundreds of sparrows flew up, out of the crack. They rose into the sky and disappeared into the clouds, and were singing a song that touched Ana's heart.

The angel opened his arms, and fire rose all around him. With his hands, he brushed the fire outward, and it spread throughout the city. It torched everything; the bodies, the homes, everything. Only she and Levi were spared.

The blue building stood untouched by the devastation, as a monument to the destruction around it.

The third angel disappeared as quickly as it came.

"Look," Ana said.

Where the sparrows rose out of the ground, a red hot lava appeared. It consumed everything: the sidewalks and buildings, even the remains of the charred bodies. The lava spread in every direction. Whatever it touched was completely consumed. Like real lava, as it moved past, the earth lay scorched in its place; scorched and barren.

Levi took her hand in his. He softly kissed it.

She could not look at him. For if she did, she would break down and start crying.

They watched the lava move through the city, until the outskirts were reached. It did not consume the reporters on the outskirts. It skipped over them.

At the point where the city ended, as if water had been poured on it, it fizzled out.

Ana looked from side to side. Where was the brown man with the snakes?

She and Levi stood for ten minutes. Yet nothing happened. In every direction there was a silence.

Finally, Ana spoke, "I think we should leave."

Still holding her hand Levi agreed, and the two rode down the elevator in silence.

They reached the ground floor, and there was

no one around.

Looking out the revolving front door, Levi said, "It's a good eight miles to get out of the city. I guess we're walking."

He felt a tap on his shoulder.

It was Ana's hand. She pointed to the corner of the lobby.

When he turned around, he saw it. In the lobby was a Vespa mini bike.

Ana held the door as he rolled it outside, where the air was thick with a smell of burning tar.

Ana got behind Levi on the bike. A path of green grass appeared before them. It was just large enough for the bike.

"The Lord will provide," Ana whispered into Levi's ear.

They drove where the path led them. At the outskirts of town, the path ended.

"Levi, stop here," Ana said.

Ana disembarked from the bike. She walked about half a block away. The image she saw was almost comical, in a sad sort of way.

Facing away from the city was a man completely encased in white cement. A large camera rested on his left shoulder, and he had one knee half bent to indicate he was trying to run.

Ana moved around him, wondering if he died quickly.

Levi joined her. Wetting his finger in his mouth, he touched the statue.

Ana looked a little shocked.

Rubbing his wet index finger across the statue,

Levi cautiously stuck it in his mouth. In a definitive voice he said, "Salt."

Ana stepped back and looked at a row of bodies. There were at least a hundred, most of those which they saw from the penthouse.

They returned to their Vespa, started off, again, and rode to locate the nearest car. They left Vespa, and got into the car. Levi drove.

Ana rested her head against Levi's shoulder. She did not know who was dead and who was alive. She knew Brother Antonio was gone. It was as if she knew the important secret, but didn't know when it was to be released.

In Lincoln Park, a suburb of Detroit outside the city, they stopped for breakfast. In the restaurant where they stopped, the TV was on.

Looking deep into his coffee, stirring it with a spoon. Levi finally blurted out, "Okay. So where is he?"

Looking up, startled, Ana asked, "Who?"

"The man with the brown body, the man with no eyes and green snakes attached to his stomach. Where is he? You saw him, you know he comes next." He leaned back against the red booth, watching the TV.

Ana pulled out her cell phone and sat next to him. The I-News channel came in the clearest, so she switched the TV channel to it.

"Once again the city of Detroit has been destroyed," the young female reporter said. "No, it was not terrorists or the criminally insane. It was an act of God. Who predicted this would happen? Ana

Caine and Levi James. Here is the MRD report and Satellite images," she said.

They watched as the images of the night before developed on her cell.

"They know our names," Levi said.

"That's the least of our problems," Ana replied.

The report continued. "We received information that the next major city to be hit will be Toledo, Ohio. The Federal Emergency Management Agency is activated, and this is what the president had to say about the current crisis."

The image flashed, and they saw the president sitting behind a desk in the White House.

"My fellow Americans. Last night our country," his voice softened. "Our world was changed forever. We are a people of God. He lives in our pledge of allegiance, in our Patriotic songs, and even in our old currency. Yet over the years we have grown away from God. We were caught up in the live for today attitude, and so we stepped over our neighbor to get something for ourselves. I am asking that today be a day of reconciliation. Go home to be with your families. Put on sackcloth or old clothes and sit with your families outside and pray for forgiveness. Those of you who are firemen, policemen, hospital workers, please continue working and pray at work. It is time for us to stand together and repent for our sins. Come together and let our Almighty God know that we are sorry. This way the people of Detroit did not die in vain. The message that was sent will live with us for the rest of our lives. Keep the families of those who were lost in your prayers and God bless America."

The young reporter came back on "So there you have it. The leader of our country is asking us to sit in sackcloth and pray. This reporter finds it all ludicrous. We don't know for sure that these large creatures are angels. They could be some kind of life from another world. Frankly, before we run off to save the world, I think we should investigate what has happened and not jump to conclusions. I'm Sue Dutter, reporting. We now return you to the net," she said.

"Cut," the director of the program said, interrupting her. "What the hell are you doing?"

The producer marched up on the set. "Aliens! Are you out of your mind?" He asked.

The reporter looked at the palm of her right hand. She watched the numbers on it glowing red.

As the producer moved next to her, she picked up her glass of water and smashed it on the table. Taking the largest shard, she thrust it into his neck, slashing his right carotid artery.

Smiling, she watched her boss bleed to death

After the newscast was over, Ana called Marie.

Marie and her friends were set up in Toledo.

Maybe the brown man won't come if the people ask for forgiveness, Ana thought. It would maybe mean that the people of Detroit did not die in vain.

"We have more work to do," Levi said, after the waitress brought their food to satisfy their ravenous appetites.

Ana's cell phone buzzed. She picked it up. Her mother called her.

"Hi, mom," Ana said. "No, I'm fine."

Her mother talked and talked, and Ana had no choice except to listen.

"Mom, I'm sorry... I love you too." She flipped her cell closed, and looked at Levi. "She wants me to come home," she said.

"I'm sure my mom would say the same thing, only with more yelling," Levi said, warmly smiling at her.

They both laughed.

Ana ran her I-card through to pay for breakfast. Putting her finger down, she put her code in, with a modest tip for the waitress.

"Let's go, Ana, and thanks for the breakfast," Levi said.

People would be looking for them, and now that she used her card, they would be able to find her.

When they walked out of the restaurant, they saw about half a dozen MRDs flying to Detroit.

Ana still had her arm linked with Levi's. The world flashed black and white, and everything faded. She tightened her grip on Levi so they would not be separated.

They came to a cliff.

Levi looked down and saw Peter with Christian.

The light flashed again, and they were back in front of the diner. They stood close, holding onto one another. Neither were able to speak.

Ana was afraid to move.

Levi rested his head against hers.

Their breathing slowed, and Levi leaned

sideways to kiss her on her forehead. There was no need for words. Only someone going through what they went through would understand the grief and pain she experienced.

He walked Ana to the car. They needed to get to Toledo to stop the destruction that surely would follow.

Levi drove out of the café parking lot, taking the car up to ninety miles per hour. Before long, they saw the signs for Toledo.

Christiant and his crew of rolling homes were headed for Ohio. He was delighting in his victory.

Some of his people died in the battle with police. They were too slow to leave the city, and suffered the fate of all those left behind.

He decided he couldn't just leave the city. He needed to see it.

Leaving the rolling homes in the suburbs, he stood on top of his rolling home with Sara, a misguided soul who slept with twenty two of the men in his rolling home.

He passed her around like currency. She was always groveling at his feet. He stood on the top of his rolling home with her on her knees in front of him. He pulled her up, and turned her around to face the city.

He rubbed her thighs and stomach. She leaned back against him. She moaned softly.

"Look, Sara, look at your reward for doing the Lord's work," he said.

An angel touched the ground, and a cold wind

came out from under his feet. It spread across the city, until it reached the outskirts.

Sara, along with everyone else, was turned to salt, with her hand reaching out in shock and amazement.

Christian laughed softly. Leaning forward, he licked the top of her head. "All I need is a margarita," he snickered.

He pushed her body off the roof. It broke into pieces when it hit the ground.

Looking to the east, he could see a few of the reporters who were also turned to salt. He howled loudly, reveling at the destruction.

He watched one of his disciples on TV redirecting the public to believe aliens had landed.

He smiled broadly. Humans would believe just about anything, he mused. By the time they figure it out, it will be too late, and then the existence of human beings will end. He would be the Lord and Master. His kind would freely roam the earth.

For millennia they hid in the shadows. The existence of Christ made it so much worse.

Then there was a ray of hope at the moment of Christ's death. The darkness that descended over the area was not God sent. It was sent by them, and before anyone could react, they pulled him into the depths of hell.

It was only for a moment, but in that short time they found the weakness in Christ. It was his mother's side, his human half. That was the moment of indecision, the indecision that sits in Church and has a split second thought that maybe God does not exist, or that Jesus is not the Lord and Savior.

The shame that surrounds that split second, the shame that God will know what you thought. That is the great power they found. All they had to do was wait for that moment. Take advantage of that moment. The result was two thousand thirty three years later. Armageddon had come.

He never told his people what Lord they were serving. The fools just assumed it was Christ. His hands glowed a deep red as he rejoiced at the death of nearly a million souls.

Once back in the rolling home, he leaned back to enjoy the ride to Ohio.

In Ohio, Marie was organizing the workers at the Saint Julie's Catholic Church, in the middle of downtown Toledo. They had signs and door hangers. Her tech team was sending emails to reach as many people as possible.

Marie lived in Detroit her whole life. She was smart enough to move her family out when they first got the message from Brother Antonio.

Dante lay asleep on a cot in the welcome center. It had been a rough two days.

Walking to McD's, she came across five people dressed in gray t-shirts and shorts. They were kneeling on the sidewalk and saying the Rosary.

Marie stopped next to one of them, a young girl in her teens.

"God bless you," Marie said.

The girl looked up at her. "If we repent, God will truly bless us," she replied.

A light bulb went on over Marie's head. Bring them to the city sidewalks, pray for forgiveness.

She walked back to the church to find a few hundred people standing in the doorway. "Hello," Marie said.

A tall dark skin man came up next to her. "Hi, I'm Reverend Joe and we are from the United Baptist Church of Cleveland. We are here to offer our services for whatever you need us to do," he stated boisterously.

Everyone cheered loudly, with an Amen or two thrown in for good measure.

"I spoke with Ana this morning. They are on their way," Marie said.

A tall young girl with large soft brown eyes and mocha colored skin, came up to her. The girl looked about twelve years old. She pulled on Marie's sleeve.

"My Aunt Sassy was in Detroit," she said. "Did she make it out okay?"

Marie smiled at her. "I'm sorry," she said "We don't know how many people made it out."

The girl brushed away some tears.

"We could not save Detroit, but we will save Toledo. We will fight to save the souls of this city. We will fight and we will end Armageddon.

Chapter Seven

Peter slept in at the Moriarty Hotel in Lambertville, Michigan. It was just over the border from Ohio.

His night had been restless. He grabbed the TV remote and put on the news. The automated news was not any longer than a commercial, so he surfed until he saw a news anchor. The news stories were longer and delivered by a person, only when there was something big going on.

"This is HJ Carpenter, channel six seventy two," a reporter said. He was showing satellite views of the city of Detroit after it had been destroyed.

"Destroyed is not the term for what has happened. This is annihilation. Every man, woman and child, even buildings and trees, all except the Sentinel Building were destroyed. The National Guard is presently on scene. Let's go to outside of Detroit. No news reporters are being allowed anywhere near the scene, so we are using MRDs to get pictures."

The image of the destruction was moved to the

cameras.

The TV focused on a man in military uniform. "I'm Captain Michael Williams of the National Guard," the man said. "As you can see, the only thing left… well, there is nothing left except one building and what looks like black asphalt."

The captain moved over to show a white pillar that looked like a man.

"We have also encountered several white rocks that look like human beings," the captain continued. "The plan is to take one back to the lab and have it analyzed."

The captain cautiously moved onto the black asphalt. He started to walk towards the blue building, when a thick fog rolled in from out of nowhere. When the fog cleared, they saw the captain was turned to salt.

The troops gasped loudly.

"Pull back!" a sergeant ordered. Turning to the MRDs the sergeant said, "We will not send anyone else out until we have more information."

It took four men to pick up the white large rock that was the captain, and secure it in the back of a large green army jeep.

The MRDs followed the truck.

The news image returned to the Anchor. "There you have it," he said somberly. "We need to do what the gospel told us to do. We need to repent for our sins and be saved."

The image went back to the home page.

Peter rose and went into the shower.

Ana and Levi arrived in Toledo. They found the nearest parking garage to the center of the city.

Ana was shaking her head back and forth.

Levi looked at her. "What is it?" he asked.

"Look at these people, going about their lives as if nothing happened," she said angrily.

Levi turned the corner to find the entrance to the parking garage.

"Look!" Ana yelled enthusiastically.

On the right side of the street were at least thirty people kneeling on mats, dressed in gray clothing, and praying.

Ana smiled at Levi and laughed softly. Her light brown hair fell loosely around her face.

At that moment, Levi knew he loved her and had to have her as his wife. "I love you," he said.

Ana's face softened. "I love you, too," she replied.

His hand covered hers and he looked deep into her dark brown eyes.

They were startled by the sound of the horn from the car behind them.

Levi slowly pulled into the garage, and the automated arm read the car's number encased in glass on the windshield.

Ana handed Levi her card, and he ran it through the parking fee meter.

They went six stories up before they found a place to park. Ten minutes later they were down on the street, walking.

Ana pulled Levi's arm, leading him to the people who were praying on the street.

"God bless you," Ana said to each of them.

Most were holding Rosaries, but they were from different creeds.

She went up and down the line, thanking them.

Even as they spoke, more people joined them.

Ana walked around the block, touching each person on the shoulder, until she ran into Marie and Dante.

"Hey," Ana said, hugging them both tightly.

"We saw the news," Marie said.

"I know. We did, too," Ana replied.

Hundreds of people came up behind Marie.

"You've been recruiting," Ana said.

Yes. I didn't have to do much, they actually found me," Marie said.

"Let's get to work. We need to watch out for the disciples of LORE," Ana said.

"What is LORE?" An older man asked.

"The Legion of Religious Elders, a group trying to hasten the Apocalypse. They are not on our side. They murdered hundreds of our people in Detroit. You can tell who they are by a mark on their right hand. It will either appear as a face or three sixes or a T on the palm of their right hand. Be on guard. Your safety is important," Ana said.

She left the people in prayer and they fanned out in the four directions to cover the entire city.

As cars stopped at the traffic lights, the people would talk to the drivers, and ask them to repent; to join them, for the day of judgment was at hand.

Between signs and pamphlets and images of

Detroit, Ana was sure they could save Toledo.

The rolling homes of LORE were parked outside the city limits, and Christian already made sure all four directions were covered.

"To victory!" he shouted.

The screaming behind him was deafening as his people marched into the city.

The satellites' view picked up the images of the two groups. Like the lines forming on a battle field, the war was imminent.

The people of LORE were handing out hundred dollar bills to anyone who would denounce the existence of God.

Even with the evidence of Detroit's destruction, they still found takers.

Anyone who would not denounce God would be punched and beaten with fists or wooden bats.

Yet, many held fast to their beliefs. If they were lucky enough to be in their cars, their cars took the brunt of the damage. Sometimes they could speed away, but sometimes they couldn't, and were forced to let their car take the beating.

Those who had no faith to begin with, would either loose nothing or find salvation at the end of the day. Either way, their choice mattered.

Every converted soul could wear white robes washed clean by the Lord. To save the city, they needed those souls to repent. Every drug addict, murderer, thief and cheater, were important.

It was difficult. A child living in poverty learned they had nothing except what the government gave them. They watched their parents lie to get help, and then spend that income on their selfish appetites.

The lesson was, if you don't steal, you will go without. Children never learn what you tell them, only what you show them.

Ana and Levi were walking through the line of cars stopped at the red light.

Suddenly, Ana leaned against a blue green VW, and had a vision. It was fuzzy at first, until it all became clear.

In Detroit, the ground was shaking in front of the great blue building. As if cut open, the ground moved and from the depths of hell arose a monster. He was fifteen feet tall, had no eyes, and just a slit to breathe through. He had a square looking head with black straw hair, wearing brown leather pants, and with a raw hide whip. A black smoke arose with him.

Attached to his abdomen were seven green snakes with baboon heads that had oversized incisor teeth. They were hungry. Many MRDs were destroyed from being too close to the creature. The green heads chomped viciously at the air.

Thousand of sparrows flew out of the ground, soaring up into the clouds.

An extremely large quantity of crows came down, landing on the white pillars of salt. Using their beaks, they pecked out the eyes of the people, which made blood pour out of the sockets where the eyes were. Then they flew in a great circle around the fifteen foot man.

The National Guard started shooting at the

snakes and the man. Lasers had no effect on him, nor did the explosive devices they tried.

People who gathered at the south end of Detroit ran for their lives, and the large crows would swoop down and attack anyone running away.

At the outskirts of Detroit, the baboon heads cut through anyone they could catch. They went through walls and ate babies in their cribs. Children playing outside became a quick snack for them. They had an insatiable hunger. The screaming was loud, sickening to hear.

A few stations cut it out of their reporting, but the MRDs that went directly online showed the carnage as it happened.

The emergency alert system went online, stopping all images from being seen. The people in other countries tried to bypass the EAS, but they were blocked out, which meant the government was responsible.

Levi came to Ana's side. "He's out, isn't he?" Levi asked.

"Yes, he is, and we are running out of time. Can you feel that?" She moved among the crowd. "Keep working everyone, please," she shouted.

Marie yelled to her. "We've lost a signal."

Ana flipped her cell open The EAS lettering came on. She scrolled through different channels and sites, but it made no difference.

"Keep working," Ana said.

Throughout the city Ana's people continued offering a means of salvation to all.

Christiant's people continued to offer money.

The two groups were moving closer and closer.

Christian, dressed in golden robes, walked down the middle of the street, waving hundred dollar bills in his hand. Before handing the money over, there was always that pesky question, "Will you denounce God?"

It was one little question that cost so much.

Back in Detroit, the great creature was corralling the green baboon snake heads, moving them in the direction of Toledo.

But every suburb south of Detroit became a feasting ground. The green baboon heads swarmed in and out of houses, ripping out walls to pull children from their bedrooms. It made a terrible crunching sound as they cut into flesh and bone.

The National Guard engaged tanks and robotic guided missiles. Their fire attack was relentless, yet when the dust settled, there was no damage to the fifteen foot man.

"How do we fight a creature sent from God?" One of the soldiers yelled.

The group turned in shocked silence to look at the soldier. But he was right. What weapon could rival the power of the Almighty?

The men forced the beast into a large apartment complex. The snakes crashed through different levels, eating people wherever they found them.

One man was waiting for his lunch to cook. With everything that was happening in the past few days, he decided to cook his favorite noodles. He was eaten by a green snake head. He'll never know how good the noodles could have been.

The green heads ate the people with no sign of being satisfied. Those who could, ran from their homes, crying and screaming, begging God to help them.

A man driving on the interstate came upon the horror of the fifteen foot man.

A young child sat on the side of the road where her mother, in an act of desperation, had thrown her. She cried and cried with crocodile tears.

A young man stopped his truck and leaped to the aid of the little girl. Picking her up, he spun around to run back to the safety of his truck.

Suddenly he froze, for around him were the green baboon snakes. Hissing and howling loudly, they stopped in their place.

From the heavens, a light shone down on the young man and the child. As quickly as they came, the monsters disappeared.

The man was standing alive and well. He kissed the little girl on her forehead.

She stopped crying when the light disappeared.

"Thank you, God," the man said loudly, as he ran to his truck.

Ana and Levi were ten blocks out when they came in contact with Christiant.

The tattooed man Ana saw at the Lighthouse, moved through the cars towards her. She never saw what happened, because it happened to fast.

Dante charged at the tattooed man.

In an instant, the man cut Dante's throat and threw him aside as if he were trash.

"No!" Ana screamed, while running to Dante's side as he bled on the street. She cradled him in her arms.

When the tattooed man came for her, Ana merely looked up, unable to move, cradling Dante's body in her arms, covered in his blood.

Suddenly, Levi knocked the man down in front of Ana. He grabbed the man's right hand.

The man burst into flames. He ran away screaming in pain. After a few seconds he fell dead.

Ana and Levi looked at each other in shock.

Then Ana had an epiphany. "We are the witnesses," she said.

"So, what does that mean?" Levi asked kneeling at her and Dante's side.

"It means we can't be harmed. As witnesses, we have to be here," Ana told him. "I see it. As a witnesses, we can use that fact as a weapon against Christian and LORE."

Ana gently laid Dante's body on the ground, folding his arms across his chest. The dark red blood saturated his hair and shoulders. Ana's pants and arms were covered in blood.

An onlooker brought her wipes, and a blanket to cover Dante.

"Thank you," Ana said.

"Attack," Christian yelled, pushing his people forward as he stayed behind.

Levi and Ana had to merely touch the disciples

of LORE to cause them to burst into flames.

Ana's people were getting hurt and killed. She wanted to tell them to retreat, but she needed to get Christian. She did not want to lose the city.

Ana worked her way through the crowds. She had a LORE disciple pinned on the ground, burning beneath her touch, and an older man wearing a suit stopped in front of her. She raised her head to look at him.

He stabbed her in her left shoulder.

Ana screamed. She laid her right hand on her assailant's face, and he burst into flames before her.

Levi came to her side.

"We have to keep going," she told him, as she held her hand against her bleeding shoulder.

Christian smiled widely with an evil grin. Taking in the pain and violence was like breathing in the smell of fresh baked bread to him.

Looking up, Christian realized Ana and Levi were coming for him. In a panic, he jumped to his feet and tried to get away from them.

Without warning, a knife was thrust into his abdomen and up into his chest. It took him a moment to focus on the face of his assailant before him. It was Peter's.

"Hello, Peter," Christian said smiling. "You know you don't have the power to get rid of me, my son."

Peter's face contorted with rage. "I am not your son!" he screamed.

Christian grabbed him by the front of his shirt, and threw him over a car.

Peter rolled over on the cement a few times before coming to a stop.

Christian pulled out the knife and was unimpressed by Peter's attempt to kill him.

Ana and Levi pushed Christian down on the hood of a car.

He laughed at them. "What do the two of you plan to do, pray me to death? Give me a piece of paper? Text me a message about salvation?"

Ana leaned over him. The blood from her shoulder wound fell into the wound on his chest and abdomen.

Smoke rose from his wound. He yelled and started fighting.

"Hold him down, Levi," she said.

She saw Peter. "Help us, Peter," she cried.

Peter held one of Christian's hands, and Levi held the other.

Ana picked up the knife Peter used to stab Christian, and cut open the left palm of her hand, letting her blood pour into Christian's wound.

A little smoke turned into a lot of smoke, and then fire.

Levi pulled Ana away as Christian burst into flames and exploded.

An MRD picked up the explosion, and then recorded the thousands of other explosions that followed.

The mark on the hands of the followers of LORE was their death sentence. All over the country, those people burst into flames and exploded.

From a satellite, it looked like a star fell to the

earth and exploded.

The death of Christiant was the death of LORE in the United States. In that one second, when the American people watched their friends and neighbors burst into flames, they stood in perfect stillness.

And in that stillness they were touched by the love of God, and by the Holy Spirit as it spread outward and upward.

Levi kissed Ana on the lips. It was a fervent kiss, and when he pulled back, Ana was smiling at him.

Her lips were pale, and she looked like she was sick. He was the last image Ana saw before she passed out.

Ana passed in and out of consciousness. In her blacked-out state, she remembered seeing Levi and Peter. She heard the alarm of the ambulance.

Then she was on a cold table with people moving around her. The next thing she remembered, she was in the morgue, lying on a cold slab. She was aware of people in outer rooms moving about the morgue.

She was alone. She tried to move her arms or legs, but couldn't. If she could yell, then they would hear her, she thought. Then they would know she was alive. She tried to yell, but couldn't.

"Think, Ana, think!" She shouted in her mind.

She saw a dark man enter the room. His suit was black with gold buttons. He had a long black beard and black eyes.

He stood over her body, and she felt ashamed that she was naked. She was afraid of this man. He picked up her left hand and pulled a knife from inside his vest.

"Go away," Ana thought, screaming inside her head. "God, make him go away!" She couldn't resist what was happening to her.

Then, where she had cut her palm to bleed on Christian, he started to cut. The pain was excruciating, and yet, she could not fight back. She was dead, and the dead were helpless against all atrocities performed upon them.

He smiled at her and his eyes glowed red.

She sat up screaming, screaming for her life.

She awoke in a bed in the hospital, with an IV in her arm, and with Levi and Peter trying to comfort her.

"Ana, Ana, it's all right," Levi said.

"It was just a bad dream, that's all," Peter said.

She looked at them, sobbing hysterically. She felt as though she had been chased by the hounds of hell. After a few minutes, she calmed down. "I want to go home," she said.

Levi left the room to find a nurse. He returned with member of the hospital staff, who brought her in a tray of food, which she devoured.

A man in a white lab coat came in. He asked her how she was feeling, and said she could be discharged.

After they took the IV out of her arm, she took a long hot shower. Thankfully, Peter brought her clothes from the hotel.

Standing in the bathroom with a large white towel around her, Ana looked at her left palm. The mirror was fogged over, but she could see a straight cut from the bottom of her middle finger to right before her wrist. "It's just a cut and nothing more," she said, scolding herself for her concern.

The mirror turned blue and there were clouds in the view. She could smell the air. The clouds, in an instant, turned black, and lightning crackled across the sky.

Then it was gone, and Ana was alone in the bathroom. As a psychologist, she knew what it meant when people hallucinated. She had seen more than what most mentally disturbed patients saw in their experiences.

Ana hoped she was not losing her mind. The dreams had been different. She knew they were not just dreams.

She folded her hands, closed her eyes, and prayed. "Please, Lord. Is this something new happening to me? I have always trusted in you, Lord, and will continue to do so. If it is for the grace of God that I should suffer, then I will do your will. In your name I pray. Amen."

Looking up at the mirror, she saw it was just a mirror, nothing more. She combed her hair and got dressed.

She looked at herself in the mirror again before she left the room, and noticed dark purple marks under her eyes. The event took its toll on her.

Coming out of the bathroom, she found Peter asleep in one chair with his mouth hanging open, and Levi sitting in the other chair watching the ball game.

Ana laughed softly. "The two of you are as exhausted as I am," she said.

Coming to her side, Levi gave her a hug and a kiss on the cheek.

"Thank God it's over," Levi said.

"Thank God," Ana said.

She had to be wheeled down to the front entrance of the hospital, but that was in accordance with hospital rules, not because of her condition.

Levi got a car, and the three returned to the hotel.

They were swamped by reporters. Levi fielded most of the questions, reassuring people the carnage was over.

They pushed their way through the crowd to the elevator.

Some of the disciples who helped the cause were still milling in and out of their rooms. They came to Ana, hugging her and Levi and Peter.

Ana kept saying, "Thank you, and God bless you."

Soon they were in their room.

"Peter, come with us to White Fish Point," Levi said.

"I can't," Peter responded. "There are other sects of LORE in other countries. I plan to expose them for what they are."

Ana closed her eyes at the thought. "Haven't we already lost enough good people?" She asked him.

"If I don't expose them, more good people will be tricked into joining them," Peter said. He kissed

Ana's cheek. "Good bye, my friends," he said.

Ana lightly kissed him, and Levi shook his hand.

"Call us every week so I know you are safe," Levi told him.

"Okay. Every week," Peter said.

They watched him leave.

"Come on, beautiful," Levi said to Ana. "It's time for us to go home."

As Ana left the room, she thought of Marie and Dante, Brother Antonio and all the good people they lost.

It was a long ride home. Thankfully, Levi did most of the driving.

Ana looked out the window at the trees that roared by. She checked her phone, and it had three thousand messages. She didn't know a phone could hold three thousand messages. She flipped it closed, and lost herself in her thoughts.

Her house was put back on the market after it was foreclosed on. Maybe she would try to buy it back, and maybe restart her practice.

Levi was a musician and a Chaplain. The hospital in White Fish point would probably take him on.

Ana was a little afraid of what would happen if she got her life back and the dreams started again. She walked away from her life once, and she wasn't sure she could do it again.

She also had some unanswered questions. The darkness that covered the world did not happen. The star falling to the Earth was actually all the people that exploded, not literally a star.

She had an uneasy feeling in the pit of her stomach. It made her think she was missing something. It was something very important, a major problem, but she could not figure it out.

Well, no matter what happened, she thought, at least she had Levi with her. Levi, who would dream the dreams with her. Levi, who would love her no matter what happened. Levi, who would be hers. She closed her eyes and let the dreams come. She was not afraid.

Chapter Eight

Seven Years Later

The alarm rang incessantly. Ana reached with one hand to shut if off.

"Hi, mommy," a tiny voice said.

Ana opened her eyes to see beautiful blue eyes of her girl, starring at her. The girl got her clear blue eyes from her father, and long flowing brown hair from her mother.

"Hello, precious girl," Ana replied, pulling her up and into the bed.

Her precious Maggie was three, and her son, named Dante, was five.

It was a fairy tale romance. In her wedding to Levi, all six of her sisters stood up and all six of his brothers did the same.

Both worked at their careers, and God blessed them not once, but twice, with beautiful babies.

The destruction of Detroit was slowly fading.

Peter was responsible for weeding LORE out of the EU, Soviet Union and China, and was busy working Africa. He came home when Dante was baptized. He was their Godfather, after all.

Ana thanked God every day for the wonderful life she had. She tickled Maggie under the covers just to hear her giggle.

"Momma, I'm gonna be late for school," a small voice said. Ana looked to see Dante standing in the doorway to her room.

"Dante, you are always so serious," Ana told him.

Dante rolled his eyes and went to the kitchen to talk to his father.

"Here's your breakfast, Dante," Levi said, placing a plate of pancakes and bacon in front of the boy.

Ana came in with Maggie in her arms. She went to Levi and received a passionate kiss.

"Hello, baby," he said to Maggie, taking her from her mother's arms. "I'll take the kids to school on my way to the hospital," he told Ana.

As Levi cut up Maggie's pancakes, Ana took a moment to appreciate the scene before her: a handsome husband with two beautiful children, a home in the city, a professional career and a beautiful day. How much had God blessed them?

Maggie spilled her OJ, which brought Ana out of her daze.

"It's okay, Maggie, just a little OJ," she said, wiping it up. She kissed the top of Maggie's head.

"Mommy, I want candy," Maggie said.

"You can't have candy for breakfast," Dante said sternly.

Levi laughed. "I'm afraid your brother is right. You can't have candy for breakfast."

After a quick shower, Ana grabbed a breakfast bar and poured coffee in her favorite black mug. "Let's go. We all have a busy day," she said.

Levi dropped Dante and Maggie at school; Dante at grammar school, and Maggie at Mother Goose Day Care, which was next to Dante's school.

He then headed to the hospital.

Ana was on her way to her office. She was stopped at a red light on Wheeler Street, and looked to her left.   There was a man leaning against a dry cleaner store. He had a black suit with gold buttons, a black beard, and long black hair.

Initially, Ana only glanced at him. Then she felt a rock in the pit of her stomach. The fear started in her stomach and traveled up to her chest. She had a tingling in her fingers, and felt like she couldn't breathe.

She slowly turned her head to get a more complete look. She had seen the man before.

A loud horn from the car behind her startled her, and she screamed. She looked again, and the man was gone.

She turned left when the light changed, and continued to her office. Her palms were sweating, and she felt like she needed to regurgitate.

She pulled into her parking spot, turned off the car, and sat with her hands glued to the steering wheel. Finally, she calmed herself enough to go upstairs.

She locked the office door behind her entry, and flipped on every light in the office. She sat at her desk and called Levi. She got his voice mail.

"This is Chaplain Levi James, I'm sorry I missed your call, but if you will leave me a message, I will get back to you as soon as possible. Thank you..." Then the beep.

"Levi, call me. It's urgent." Ana closed her phone and started looking through her patient list for the day.

"I'll stay busy, so the day will go quickly," she said aloud. Her first patient would arrive in ten minutes. She put together her charts for the day, and made sure they were in order.

She started the day by seeing Donna Meickle. When she initially saw her, she was a fourteen year old freshman in high school.

A girl sitting next to her accidentally moved her hand onto Donna's desk. Donna took a stylus and stabbed it into the girl's hand. Blood squirted out of the girl's hand, and she had to be taken to the emergency room.

Donna not only did the stabbing, but she showed no remorse for her actions.

Ana really struggled to get Donna to open up. Her mother died when she was two. Her father was a good man, but he didn't show emotions well. He was beyond being very reserved. There was no other ancillary family. So the two of them muddled through life alone.

When Ana finally got Donna to open up, she got Donna's her dad in for counseling. Over a six week period, dad and daughter really talked about what they were feeling inside. It was a three hankie affair. He cried, Donna cried, and Ana cried. It was a wonderful day for all of them.

She continued to see Donna for reinforcement, since Donna needed a strong female influence in her life. There were social situations that came up and dealings with boyfriends she needed to address.

Ana's cell rang. "Hello," she said, answering it.

"Honey, what's wrong?" Levi asked her.

Ana could hear the worry in his voice. Should she tell him, or should she not?

"Levi, I'm sorry I scared you, but I saw the man from my dream," she said. Honesty was the best policy, she decided.

"Are you sure?" he asked

"Yeah, I'm sure." Any normal person would scoff at a man from their dream, but not the two of them.

"I was driving and I saw him, but more than that, I felt him. Then the car behind me beeped the horn. I looked at it, and when I looked back, he was gone." She tried to keep her voice calm.

"Let me finish up with this family, and I'll come over," Levi told her.

"No, no I'm fine just talking to you. It's okay now, honey. If anything else comes up, I will call you immediately," she said to reassure him.

She flipped her cell phone closed, and leaned back in her chair. She could not remember the dreams from before the war. They had been so important, so crystal clear in every detail, but over time a fog moved into her brain and shrouded the dreams from her.

Sometimes she would reread the dream she posted, just to remind herself it did happen. The images would hide in her normal dreams, just around the corner from the happy pleasant dreams. The only thing she could always remember was the man in the morgue.

Sometimes she was walking in her dreams with her children. The sun was shining and the grass was green. She would put them on the grass and around the corner the sky would darken. She didn't always see him, but she knew he was there. She hated that she would forget her dreams within minutes of waking. Maybe God does that on purpose, otherwise your waking life would be less productive than your dreaming life.

She should know that. Her dreaming life became her obsession. Waking or sleeping, it didn't seem to matter. Being a psychologist, She knew that sometimes dreams were the mind trying to correct the issues not completed while awake. Sometimes dreams were just dreams, like cigars were just cigars.

There was a knock on the door, which brought Ana back to reality. It was Donna.

Ana let her in, and smiled at her warmly. "Let's get started," she said.

Ana was busy the rest of the day. The image of the man was put on the back burner. She had her young adults in the mornings and children in the afternoon.

She had a new patient. He was court ordered

to see her, which was not unusual. She had a good amount of court ordered patients. What made him unusual was he was in Juvenile Detention. He was twelve years old. He had killed his parents and his younger sister.

Ana had a few kids under house arrest or on probation. She had a circuit court judge friend who really felt Ana had great success with troubled kids. He personally called her and asked if she would see this boy.

Ana flipped on her recorder when the boy came in through the door. She was surprised to find a police escort with the boy, handcuffed to him.

"Ma'am," the officer said.

"Hi, it's nice to meet you," Ana said to both of them.

The police officer led the boy into the room. "Where do you want him?" he asked. It sounded like he was delivering furniture.

"The chair right there is fine," Ana said.

The large burly man sat the boy in the chair, and handcuffed him to the brown wooden hand rest on the chair.

"Where do you want me?" the cop asked.

"Well, the waiting room is fine," Ana replied.

The cop came closer to her. "Listen, lady," he said. "You seem real nice, but you have to remember, this kid stabbed his mother twenty seven times after killing his father. You can't trust him."

"We'll leave the door open. Then you can see me," she said. "If there is any problem, I'll scream my head off. Okay?" Ana smiled at him.

"Okay," he begrudgingly replied, and left the office.

Ana sat in the chair across from the boy. To look at him, he seemed like a regular twelve year old. He was mulatto with curly black hair and large brown eyes. He was nearly six feet tall with a medium build.

"My name is Ana," she said. "I know you're Marcus Jones and you're doing time at the Addison JD Home. All I want to do is talk to you and help you sort through any issues that you feel you have," she added in the softest, kindest voice she had.

He may not even speak to her today, Ana thought. It took three sessions before Donna would say even one word to her. Ana knew patience was a must with these types of kids.

The boy sat looking at his feet.

Ana relaxed. "We can just sit here or we can play v-games if you like." Boys loved v-games a lot more than girls.

He sat looking at his shoes, so Ana sat back and waited. After about five minutes, the boy said something unintelligible.

"I'm sorry," Ana said leaning in closer.

"What kind of games do you have?" he asked.

Ana smiled at him warmly. "Let's look," she said.

Soon, she and Marcus were playing Defcon 4 and the child in Marcus quickly emerged. He started to have fun. For the first forty-five minutes, they played the game. Then Ana said they had to do a little work.

"If I come here, can I play the game every time?" He asked in a pleading voice.

"Definitely. For forty-five minutes we can play, and then talk for fifteen," Ana told him.

"Okay, then I'll come here," Marcus said.

Ana used this technique before with kids. Over time, they would want to talk more and play less.

"So, Marcus, can we talk about what happened? I'm not here to judge you or trick you. This is just a safe place for you to come and talk."

"You won't believe me," Marcus said. "No one does," he looked at his shoes again.

"Try me," Ana said placing her hand over his.

His face turned a crimson red and then tears fell. He was blubbering when Ana brought Kleenex crouching down next to him.

"It was a man. He made me do it," Marcus said.

"Slow down, Marcus, I can't understand you." Marcus laid his head against her shoulder.

She looked up to see the officer peering into the room. "I'm okay," Ana said to him.

He went back to the waiting room.

By then Marcus had stopped crying. "Tell me again," Ana said patiently.

The boy returned to his story. "There was a man. I would see him out of the corner of my eye. When it started, I saw him once in a while, but then it was all the time. I would be standing by a fence, watching my friends play basketball. Then I would hear his voice in my ear."

"What would he say?" Ana interjected.

"He would tell me that my father wanted to get rid of me."

"Is there any truth to what he was saying?" Ana asked.

"I found out a week earlier that I was adopted. We had a big fight and I ran out of the house," he said. "I came back, but I wouldn't talk to my dad. Then I started sensing the bad man in my room. I would wake up in the middle of the night and know he was there. I couldn't shut him out. I don't even remember killing my family. I remember being asleep, and the next thing I knew, I was standing in the living room holding a carving knife with blood every where. My sister, my mom, my dad, all dead, killed by me."

Ana played the tape of his call to 911.

"I called in the murder, but I don't remember it," he said to Ana.

She knew this was transference, to blame an unknown assailant.

"Okay," Ana said. "Tell me about the man."

Marcus pulled a piece of folded paper out of his pants and handed it to Ana.

She slowly opened the paper. "Can I keep this?" Ana asked.

"Yes... You know who this is, don't you?" Marcus asked her.

Ana looked up at him, "Our session is over," she said. After standing up, she called in the officer.

"Please help me," Marcus said as the officer walked him out of the office.

Ana placed the picture in her attaché case. It held her laptop files and CD's. She walked down the stairs to her car.

She turned the key and pushed the start button, and soon she was off. It had been a long day. She looked forward to being home with her babies. That always rejuvenated her.

When the car came to a stop for a light or stop sign, her neck would become rigid. If she did not turn her head, she would not see anyone.

She pulled into the driveway, and breathed a sigh of relief. She went inside her house, and was greeted by her little Maggie.

"Mommy, mommy, mommy. You're home." Her little legs ran as fast as they could.

Ana put down her attaché case, and picked up her little bundle of joy.

She went into the kitchen to see her husband cleaning up the dishes. "Hi, Hon," she said, giving him a kiss.

"I have your food in the micro," he said.

She definitely was hungry.

She opened the micro door, and saw macaroni and cheese, hot dogs, and green beans. She pushed the one minute timer button, and placed Maggie down.

"Where's Dante?" Ana asked.

"In his room doing his homework." Levi replied.

Ana went in to check on Dante.

Hi honey," Ana said, giving him a kiss on the head.

"Hi, mom," he said.

"How was school?" she asked.

"Fine. We are learning nouns and verbs," he said. Looking at his learning pad, he would touch the noun and put it with the correct definition.

"You're doing a great job. How much more homework do you have to do?" she asked.

"Three more pages like this, not too much," he said.

She gave him another kiss on the top of his head, and went back into the kitchen.

Maggie sat on her lap while she ate.

Levi was telling her about his day. An older man passed away and the family started arguing about property rights and belongings. Levi told her that people reacted differently to death. For some, it was a moment to come together. For others it caused rifts in the family to become wider. It was a shame to see how badly people acted. Levi said he sometimes was faced with knock down drag out fights. The police actually had to be called to the hospital to stop the fights, sometimes.

They watched some TV after Ana finished dinner. Maggie loved the kiddie program with bears. She would jump up and down on her parent's bed for half the program.

Dante lay on his stomach with his hands tucked under his chin, and Maggie's bouncing would occasionally land on him, which would make Dante call their mom.

Ana told Maggie not to jump on the bed.

Maggie cried to Levi, who would tell her she could jump on the bed, but not to jump on her brother. Then the whole process would start over.

At eight thirty, Maggie and Dante went to bed. Then, and only then, would Ana and Levi talk about problems.

Ana did not want her children exposed to the horrors of the world, and many of her patients truly had horrors in their past.

She filled Levi in about Marcus, and pulled out the sketch of the man. She took the small key off her long necklace and opened the locked door on her brown wood desk.

She pulled the printed dream from seven years ago. No one printed on paper any more. It was too expensive, but Ana wanted a copy of her dream she could hold in her hands.

Beneath the papers was a larger paper that Ana picked up carefully. She sat on the bed with Levi and slowly opened the paper. She compared the two drawings. The only difference was that in Ana's drawing, the man had red eyes.

"What does it mean?" Levi asked her.

"I don't know. I just don't know," she said.

Ana was exhausted from work, so when they went to bed, she gratefully fell asleep right away.

Levi got up, checked the locks and looked outside the windows to make sure there were no intruders.

Both the kids were asleep.

Levi channeled surfed for a while. What was happening? He asked himself. Could the man in the drawings make Ana kill her family, or make someone else do it?

Levi found himself praying for help. The truth

was, Levi was afraid the blessings of his life would be taken from him, that evil would find him, and his wife and family. He decided he would stop by the church and see

Father John. Soon, he fell asleep with the TV on.

For the first time in seven years, Ana dreamed. Not the dreams that one forgets, but the real dreams.

She was dressed in a white gown, standing in a spot light. It was the only light she could see. She looked around for Levi, but could not find him.

She looked into the darkness. She couldn't see anything, but she knew something was there. She sensed it.

She folded her arms under her breast, and hugged herself tightly. She prayed the 'Our Father' under her breath, as she kept looking into the darkness.

Then a small isle full of light opened, and Ana was compelled to walk down it. She was amazed at how dark it was around her. There were no reflective images at all.

In front of Ana was a door. The door was white and made of pine. Her curiosity got the better of her. She touched the white door and the white frame around it. It was just plain white wood.

She took in a deep breath, and moved her finger on what she thought would be a wall to which the door was connected. But there was no wall, just empty space.

She pulled her fingers back in pain. The tips of her first three fingers were frozen and blue. She curled up her hand, and blew into it, hoping to warm her frozen fingers.

She turned the silver knob on the door and slowly pushed it open.

The isle of light led her into the center of the room. The room lit up, and she found herself in Detroit, in the center of the blackened ground.

What she saw wasn't the Detroit of her present day. A memorial was built in the center of the city. Ana never returned to Detroit, but online she saw the memorial. The inscription on it simply read:

> "Friends and Neighbors pass me by,
> As you are now so once was I,
> As I am now you soon shall be,
> Prepare for death and follow me."

Underneath that it read:
> "For all the souls lost on this last
> battleground of Earth."

It listed all the people who were lost. The reporters had their own section.

In the Detroit she saw in her dream, there was no memorial. It was empty, with no one around.

She waited for someone to come, to explain what she was supposed to do. She walked to the edge of the darkness. She peered as hard as she could into the darkness.

Then she saw eyes peering back.

At first, there were two red ugly eyes with black pupils. Then they multiplied; four, then eight. Then the darkness became alive with all the eyes watching her.

She instinctively moved away from the darkness. She looked around to see if anything else was different. What was she supposed to do?

The light around the city became smaller.

Ana quickly moved to the center of the light.

Slowly the light moved inward.

Ana stood perfectly still.

As the light moved, so did the eyes.

Coming ever closer, Ana waited for the darkness to encompass her. She could hear clicking, a loud clicking like hundreds of claws hitting the ground.

She was afraid, and then the light was over her body and the eyes were within her reach.

A claw came into the light and hooked onto her gown. Smoke rose from the top of the claw as the light ignited it. It burst into flame.

She tried to pull back away from the claw, but it was too strong and it pulled her into the darkness.

Levi awoke to Ana's screaming. "Honey, you're okay. You're okay," he said.

It took a minute for her to calm down. She was shaking and crying. Most of what she said to him in explanation, initially, was garbled at best.

After a drink of ice water, she was calm enough to tell him the dream.

He looked at her long white night gown and picked it up in the center to show Ana. It was ripped for about two inches, and was also burned.

They looked up at each other in shock.

"What is happening?" Ana asked.

"I don't know," Levi replied.

It took a while, but Levi finally got Ana back

to sleep.

Levi was soon back asleep with a protective arm around Ana's body.

The clock ticked, and all was quiet in the house. Then Ana dreamed she was up in her white night gown. She was unsure if she were awake or asleep, though she was hoping she was awake.

She was in a house that was not her own. Inside was a little girl, asleep.

Looking at the little girl sleeping so soundly, she was reminded of her little Maggie.

Ana heard a muffled cry and went to investigate.

In a great room, a large black man lay bleeding on the carpet. The butcher knife was still in his back. His wife beside him was still alive, pulling herself towards her husband. She was bleeding too much to make it to him. Soon, she bled out and died on the blue carpet.

Ana saw Marcus come in the door with his father's gun. Stepping over his mother's body, he headed to the bedroom.

Ana couldn't understand why Marcus held a gun, and not the knife he used in the real murders.

"Marcus!" Ana called. "Marcus!"

He did not respond.

Ana followed him to his sister's bedroom. She tried to grab his arm, but there was no substance to him, and her hand passed though him.

"Marcus, please listen to me," she said.

Raising the gun, Marcus' hand shook as if he were trying not to shoot the gun. But, the gun fired, and the bullet went into his little sister's brain. She didn't cry out; it was an instantaneous death.

Marcus went back to the living room and dropped the gun on the ground.

A great cry came from deep within Marcus.

Ana watched as a creature came from inside Marcus. It had great claws on its hands and feet. It was a slick black creature, with the face of a dog and sharp white teeth.

After it left Marcus, the boy lay unconscious on the living room carpet.

As it moved towards Ana, she heard the clicking sound of its claws on the kitchen floor, and saw the red eyes watching her. It moved past her and out the door.

Ana opened her eyes to find Levi next to her. She turned on her side and pulled the comforter over her.

Levi half awakened, pulled the covers back.

When Ana opened her eyes the next time, it was because the alarm was going off and it was morning. She went into the bathroom, and updated Levi about her second dream.

"So, Marcus is innocent," Levi said.

"Yes, but how do we prove it?" Ana asked him.

"I don't know," Levi said.

"I keep wondering why Marcus? How did they choose Marcus? If I can figure out why, then maybe we can help him," she said.

Ana pulled out her red tooth brush and brushed her teeth.

There was a knock on the door, and Ana opened it to see Dante waiting patiently there.

"Hi, sweetie," Ana said.

"Hi mom. Do you want me to make breakfast today?" He asked.

Ana laughed softly and she heard Levi laughing from the shower.

"What kind of breakfast are you planning?" Ana asked.

"Just cereal and milk," he replied.

"Okay. Cereal it is," Ana said.

Levi and Ana switched places as Ana got ready for work.

Dante was such a great kid, Ana thought. He was very serious and had always been that way. Even as a baby, he would study anything put in front of him. His heart was undeniable. He was kind to everyone, including his little sister. He definitely takes after Levi.

In contrast, Maggie was the hugs and kisses girl. She was also the only one who could hug and kiss Dante, and he wouldn't squirm away. They adored each other, and Ana was grateful for that.

The morning went quickly, and when Ana arrived at the office she made a note to herself that she had not seen the mysterious man that morning.

She settled in the office for a good twenty minutes before her first appointment.

Ana pulled out Marcus' disc and opened it on her lap top. The title flashed before her eyes: 'Confidential Records of the Circuit Court of White Fish Point._

The next screen was a disclaimer. It said the information is confidential and not to be looked at by any unauthorized personnel. It had everyone of Marcus' court dates and hearings.

Ana looked through every word, every picture, and every excerpt.

The trial went quickly. Marcus did not contest anything. He merely sat in the courtroom day after day with a lost look on his face.

Ana felt so bad for him. He wasn't a bad kid.

She saw his grades from school. Mostly Bs, with a love of math and science. He was born in White Fish Point. It was also there that he was baptized, made his first communion, and where he made his Reconciliation. There was nothing about him that was different, or unusual.

"It's something in front of me and I can't see it," Ana said out loud.

She put things away in time for her first patient.

At one o'clock she checked in on Maggie and Dante with a video looker. Afterwards, she called Levi, who was very busy at the hospital, so he promised to pick up dinner.

Then she went back to work. At five thirty, she finally backed up her files and locked up the office.

Her stomach was growling so loud, it worried her a little.

She stopped at the red light. She looked across the street, and saw a young man who looked like Marcus.

She shook her head. Marcus was locked up. My

eyes must be playing tricks on me, she thought.

Before she knew it, she was home, eating Chinese food, with Maggie jumping up and down on her lap.

Ana ran her fingers through Maggie's curls. "Hi baby," she said, kissing Maggie's neck.

Maggie giggled and squeezed her tight.

"How was school, Dante?" Ana asked.

"It was good. We are doing some adding and subtracting," he said.

"Great, I love adding and subtracting," Levi added.

"Me, too," Dante said very seriously.

Ana smiled at him warmly. "That's my boy," she said.

Chapter Nine

Ana was in bed, watching reruns and channel surfing as Levi slid beneath the covers. He kissed Ana on the lips passionately.

"Sweet dreams," he said. "Wake me up if you have any problems"

She returned the kiss. "You will be the first to know," she said.

Ana was soon asleep, and dreaming.

She opened her eyes, and was in a place she did not know. It was bright and beautiful. There were white pillared buildings but it was something more. Everything sparkled as if recently polished.

She walked toward a building to the left of her, and saw a waterfall near grass; a scene of blue and green.

To the right of her were trees that looked like weeping willows, but with white vines with silver and blue flowers.

Walking up some marble steps, she found a door. It opened, and out came Brother Antonio.

Ana rushed to him and embraced him tightly.

"I am so sorry I could not do more to save you," she said.

"Everything is as it should be," he said, hugging her tightly. "The message you gave is even more important today," he added. "The world exists the way it is suppose to. There is day and there is night. There is good and there is evil. There is light and there is darkness. What happened to Marcus is called a dark tear. It is a rip in the light. A weakness that allows the darkness to come through," he told her.

Ana's mind was racing. "How do we close up the holes?" She asked.

"Remember the message. You have all the power you need," he said.

Ana was being pulled back, away from Brother Antonio. "Remember both the messages," she heard him say from far away.

Ana awoke in her bed. It was two thirty in the morning. The second message was 'everything begins and ends with the will of God.' She would have to figure that out tomorrow, she told herself, as she closed her eyes. The rest of her sleep was peaceful and uninterrupted by dreams.

The alarm was incessantly ringing as Ana reached for the snooze button.

"Hey, girl. Rise and shine," Levi yelled from the bathroom.

She hated how cheerful he was in the morning.

"How was your night?" he asked.

"Actually, it was very productive." Ana said, half stumbling to the bathroom. "I saw Brother Antonio, and he told me there are dark tears where evil can come through. He also said the messages are very important."

Levi stuck his head out of the shower. "The messages?" he asked.

"Yes, so you have to help me figure this out," she told him.

Ana made instant pancakes for breakfast. As always, it was a rush to get everyone off to school and work.

Ana was contemplating her issues in life. She tended to leave things behind her. She would cut off parts of her life and never look back: Previous boyfriends, college friends, people from back home. She never really kept in touch with anyone.

Her sisters were not like that. Nor were her mom or dad. Logically, she realized she was doing it, but didn't know why.

Even in Detroit she was invited many times to speak at the memorial. The southern suburbs had also set up a memorial, and Ana could not bring herself to go. Not going and speaking made things final, in her mind, and she believed that was a good thing.

Ana parked her car, and walked up the steps to her office. As she put the key in her office door, she heard a voice behind her.

"Ana," the voice said.

Ana jumped and turned to see Donna. She was sobbing hysterically and threw herself into Ana's arms. Her incoherent speech between sobs was not working. Ana guided her into the office and sat her down on the red waiting room sofa.

"I don't know what happened," Donna cried.

"He was fine, and then he just snapped," she told Ana.

"Who," Ana asked, dreading to hear the answer.

"My dad," she cried.

"Where is he now?" Ana asked.

"At the house, I think," Donna replied.

Ana flipped open her cell phone,

Wait, who are you calling?" Donna asked.

"The police," Ana replied.

"Please don't call the police. The person in my house was not my dad. Please, Ana. I don't want him arrested," she cried.

"Okay," Ana said. Any other time she would have called the police immediately. But after the last few days, she was worried it really wasn't her father.

"I am going to call my husband in case we need help," she said.

Ana did a 911 text to Levi and gave him Donna's address.

"One sec," Ana said. Pulling out the record for her patients, she grabbed a 'will be back' sign to hang on the door.

Marcus' file was just below it in the drawer. His address was ninety seven ten Western road.

Donna's address was ninety eight twenty one Western road. They were a block apart.

"We'll take my car," Ana said.

She opened the door for Donna, then slid into the driver's seat.

"Donna, did you know a boy named Marcus

who lived by you?" She asked cautiously. She could lose her license for releasing information.

"You mean the boy who killed his family? Everyone knows him," Donna replied.

"I know you're older, but what was he like?" Ana asked?

"He was a nice kid, He was actually, really nice. Jonathon, who lived two doors down from me, broke his bike and he had to walk to school and then to work. Marcus gave him his old bike for free! It really was crazy that he killed his family," Donna said emphatically.

When Ana turned the corner onto Donna's block, the sky became very black with dark rolling clouds and lightning streaks across the heavens.

"Oh my, look at those clouds," Ana said.

Giving her a strange look, Donna said, "What are you talking about? The sky is beautiful."

It became Ana's turn to be puzzled.

"My house is the one on the left with the brown fence," Donna said.

Ana pulled into the driveway. She and Donna cautiously got out. Ana was hoping Levi would arrive soon.

Linking arms with Donna, they walked to the front door. The sky was changing from a black color to a black and purple color. They stood at the front door together. Ana took one last look down the street for Levi, then the two went inside.

The living room was empty with only wood floors and green and white couches. Nothing seemed out of place.

The two slowly moved into the kitchen.

Donna's father lay on the floor, starring up at the ceiling.   Ana went to his side. He appeared to be unharmed.

"Joe," Ana said softly. She put a hand across his forehead. White foam came from his mouth, and spilled down his neck and chest. He made a sound like an animal dying. A light came from inside him, and a creature sprang from his body. It ran past them and into the back room.

"Is he all right?" Donna asked, apparently unaware of what Ana was seeing.

"He'll be fine. Come and sit with him," Ana told her.

The front door opened and Levi came in.

"Thank God," Ana said. Pulling him to the back room, she filled him in.

"Did you see that sky out there?" he asked her.

"I hate to break it to you, but we may be the only ones who see it," Ana replied. She turned the light on in the back bedroom.

"Look, do you see it?" Ana asked.

Against the far wall next to a long dresser were two black tear drops as big as a man's hand.

"Don't touch them," Levi said to her.

She knew what they did to Joe and had no intention of touching them. She held up her right hand close to the teardrops, and closed her eyes. She opened herself to the spirit. She prayed for help. Ana felt a warmth and tingling sensation throughout her body.

Then the teardrops shrunk in the sight of the

light.

Ana opened her eyes to find the black teardrops were gone.

"Somehow, these creatures are coming through to our world, through the black teardrops," Ana said. "Marcus lives on the next block," she added.

"Call an ambulance for your dad," she called to Donna.

Donna flipped open her cell phone, and called.

Levi and Ana moved cautiously together from room to room, searching, but there were no more teardrops.

"I want to go to Marcus' house," Ana said.

"Okay," Levi replied.

Walking through the house, Ana stopped to reassure Donna before they headed for the street where Marcus' house stood.

"It seems like the darkness is at its worse over this house," Levi said.

Ana nodded in agreement.

Slowly turning around, Ana noticed that the sky was blue again over Donna's house.

"Come on," Levi said.

They went in the house together. In the living room, they saw the blood soaked brown carpet. It looked like ten people died here, not two.

"Do you see it?" Ana asked.

"No, but let's keep going," Levi told her.

The bathroom was clean, and the back bedroom where the little girl died was clear.

Ana pulled Levi to Marcus' bedroom. They found four black teardrops. Two on the back wall over Marcus' bed and two on the wall to the left of the door. They looked like pools of black water.

Ana moved to the back wall first, getting only as close as she dared. She held up her hand, focusing on the light that lived inside her.

Levi watched as Ana's hand glowed white, and light poured forth.

The teardrops shrunk until there was nothing left.

She turned her attention to the side wall, making quick work of the black teardrops there.

They quickly checked out the rest of the house, including the garage, and not finding any more black teardrops, they left.

The sky above them was blue with soft white clouds, and the sun shone a white light that cascaded over the houses.

Levi walked Ana back to her car, and they returned to Donna's house.

Inside, the ambulance an EMT was working on Donna's father.

Donna was busy talking to the police.

Ana made a signal to Donna, and Donna waved her a good by.

"I have to get back to the office. My patient is probably pacing in front of my door," she said.

"You know they will figure out that we are stopping them," Levi said. "They may come for us. Maybe we should send the kids to your mom's."

Ana had a pained look in her eyes. She really had not thought that there could be consequences for their actions. "We will have to talk about this tonight," she said.

She kissed his cheek, and headed off to work. She knew for sure that Marcus was innocent, yet in the eyes of the law it didn't matter. There was no 'possessed by a demon' clause in the law.

There must be a way to help Marcus, she thought. She would come up with something. Her mind was reeling as she pulled into her parking spot at the office.

A wave of anger came over her. She gripped the steering wheel as if it were her lifeline. She was so angry, she screamed as loud as she could. She hit the steering wheel with her fists and she tossed her head side to side. She was sure she looked like a crazy woman. The problem with demons was supposed to be over. She had given up everything to follow the Word of God, but the evil wasn't over.

Even though it was a great sacrifice, she was called and she answered. It took more than two years for her to get her life back to normal. For the first six months, she had MRDs flying everywhere. She was bombarded by the press. She even had people pretending to need help, when all they wanted was an interview.

The worst of it all was the hundreds of people who lived outside the Lighthouse, sitting in sackcloth.

Ana brought the world back to God and back to Jesus, even though the cost was high. All the people who died. It took so long for her to get her life back. Was it all starting over again?

Slowly, she gained control over her breathing

and her emotions. Luckily, no one was around to see her behavior.

She closed her eyes, and prayed for understanding, for patience. She prayed for strength. She prayed for her children. If God's plan included her, then she must do what the Lord needed her to do

When Ana opened her eyes, Tim was standing in front of her car, waving to her. He was her eleven thirty appointment.

Sighing heavily, Ana got out of her car and headed inside. They walked up the stairs together.

At one p.m., after she was finished with Tim, Ana grabbed lunch from one of the v-machines. It was a chicken salad on rye sandwich, with grapes and water.

When Marcus was brought in, Ana had to control herself.

The guard was the same from two days ago.

After putting one of the handcuffs on the wooden chair, the guard gave her the same speech.

"I feel that leaving the door open makes Marcus feel inhibited about discussing what happened," she said. "I would like to close the door to speak to him." She gave the guard her best smile. "However, if there is any problem, I will scream loudly."

The guard shrugged his shoulders and went out to the waiting room.

Ana rushed to Marcus' side.

Startled, he rolled back in the chair.

In a soft hushed voice she said to him, "Don't be afraid. I know what happened the night your family died. You were taken over by a demon. I can't come out to the authorities and say that, so we need to circumvent the problem. I spoke with the Catholic Church, and gave them this information. They will have a lawyer come to see you. He will re-open your case and try to reduce or eliminate your sentence."

Ana breathed in, tired from talking so much. Looking up into his face, she saw tears cascading down his cheeks.

"I didn't kill them?" he asked.

"No, it was this creature, the demon, that took you over. That is why you passed the lie detector test," Ana said.

Grabbing onto Ana, he pulled her close against his chest, and hugged her while crying like a baby. The flood gates opened, and all the pain poured out through the tears he shed.

"It will be all right," Ana told him.

"Why? Why me?" He asked.

"I don't know at this time, but I will do my best to get answers for you," she replied.

At the end of their session, Marcus stood with his head held high and kissed Ana's cheek before leaving.

Ana left her office, jumped into her car, and headed home. There was no sign of the man she saw in the morgue.

It was five thirty when Ana finally made it home. The kids were eating spaghetti and Maggie had it everywhere. Her brown hair looked more like spaghetti than hair.

In contrast, Dante was perfectly clean with his

napkin tucked into his blue school shirt.

Levi kissed Ana's cheek as he came in with her dinner.

"Thank God you can cook," Ana said laughing.

"Maggie enjoys my cuisine," Levi told her.

After the kids were tucked in for the night, Levi and Ana could finally sit and talk.

"That was a great idea, getting the church involved," Levi told her.

"If anyone can help him, they can," Ana replied.

"What about the darkness? How will we know how much is around? We are the only ones who can see the darkness," Levi said. "We need a plan, and we need it right now," he added.

"I still think we are missing something, but I don't know what it is," Ana said.

She was exhausted, and soon fell asleep in the arms of her husband.

In a dream, Ana awoke in the white spot light with the darkness all around. She could sense that the darkness was not empty.

The isle of white light appeared.

She cautiously moved down the isle of white light. Again, the pine white door appeared at the end of the isle. She knew better than to try to touch anything beyond the sides of the white door. She didn't want her fingers to get frozen.

She turned the silver door knob, and pushed the door open. She stopped. She had an epiphany. Perhaps walking through the doorway was a choice.

There are millions of choices we make in life and we decide what those choices and consequences are. Should I walk through the door or should I choose to stay here?

She heard a click behind her, and the light shut off. She heard growling and moaning behind her.

No time for an epiphany, she thought. She needed to go now, she decided.

She fell upon entering the door and as she looked back, the spot of light disappeared.

The room became illuminated, and she was back in Detroit, on the blackened asphalt, which was all that remained of the living part of the city.

She moved to the center of the city. Darkness closed in around her. Panicked, she held up her right hand to protect herself.

A white light that came out of her hand, and the darkness retreated.

She could hear the clicking of nails on the ground. She felt a strange itching and burning on her left hand. Slowly, she turned her left hand up so she could see it. The scar that healed seven years ago was glowing red.

She flashed back to the moment with Christiant. The knife she picked up to cut her hand was the same knife Peter used to stab Christiant. His blood and hers had co-mingled. She was infected by him!

As she returned from her flashback, a large black creature grabbed onto her gown and was attempting to pull her into the dark.

Ana awoke screaming and crying. Levi could not comfort her. She jumped out of her bed getting tissue to wipe her eyes. Then she went to the garage and opened tool boxes and gardening sets.

"What are you looking for?" Levi asked.

"An axe!" She yelled at him. She found it in the bottom drawer. She ran back into the kitchen and placed her left hand on the table.

Levi came from behind as she raised the ax over her head. He grabbed the axe from her and spun her around.

"For the love of God, what are you doing?" he asked.

"If your hand offends God, cut it off," she said.

Levi sat her down, not understanding her.

She told him about the dream.

Levi opened her left hand, touching the healed scar. "When Peter found me and we burned the face off my hand, I felt redeemed. I went to meet Christian of my own accord. This was not your choosing. This was to save the world," he said.

Ana was flustered. "Who is this man, then? Why are Marcus and I seeing the same man?"

"Have you ever looked at Marcus' hand, or the hand of his parents? Could they have belonged to LORE?" he said.

She shook her head.

I will call Peter in the morning. He has a list of all LORE members in the US and EU," Levi said. "And you are not cutting off any parts of your body!"

He took the axe to the garage and hid it. He returned to the kitchen and helped Ana back to bed.

The rest of the night was uneventful. Ana got what she really needed, a restful sleep.

Levi called Peter in the morning.

Peter promised to look up the information. Soon they were all out the door, off to school and work.

Ana called the judge who assigned Marcus to her, and asked for the autopsy report on Marcus' parents.

He was a little concerned about turning over autopsy reports, but Ana explained that sometimes more intimate information about the crime could help the child see what was done.

Whatever she said, worked. The courts sent a courier to deliver the report.

Ana anxiously looked through the report. The mother had a tramp stamp that read 'hottie', but no marks were on her hands. That ruled her out.

The father, however, had a face image on his palm. He had not been activated, otherwise his palm would have had three six's, instead.

Ana thought everyone in the Michigan area was activated on that day the world went crazy.

People all over the U.S. killed their babies, their parents, and their pets, without remorse. Some people as far away as San Antonio became crazy.

One man strangled his eighty two year old mother.

So why is it that Marcus' dad was not activated? Also, why was it not his father who went crazy and killed his family? That would have made more sense.

Ana had even more questions without

answers.

A tall blonde stewardess responded to the light in first class. "Can I help you sir?" she asked.

Peter smiled at her with a gorgeous smile. "Yes, miss. Can I get a soda, please?"

"Certainly," she replied.

It was a beautiful day, and Peter looked forward to setting his feet in his own country. After learning from Levi what was happening, he had no choice but to return home. After all, he was Dante's Godfather.

The real truth lay in the tone of Levi's voice. He was afraid, and Peter was worried about all of them. He owed his life to Ana and Levi. More than that, he owed his soul to them. Meeting Levi and talking to him put the seed of doubt in his mind. That seed grew, and he saw the truth for what it was before it was too late. If they were in need, he would be there.

Ana hung up the phone after talking to her husband. She held up both of her hands, examining the palms. On Ana's right were twelve stars in a circle.

On Ana's left palm was the scar where she cut herself to destroy Christian. Perhaps she should send Maggie and Dante away. Her mother would love to take them, so would all her sisters and Levi's brothers and parents.

What if the darkness got into her? She could do things without even knowing she did them.

As she sat lost in thought, her cell phone went off, startling her. The caller was her last appointment for the day. He was calling to cancel.

Ana explained the risk of canceling. His court appointed parole officer would issue a warrant for him. That was the rule with all parolees she saw.

He said his daughter was sick and he was at the hospital.

"Well, that is a different matter. When you check in, ask them to email me that your child is in the hospital," Ana said.

"Well," he stammered, "what if she doesn't get admitted."

"That doesn't matter. As long as you're in the hospital, they will email me. Just give them my name," she said.

The man became angry. "Fine. That's what I'll do," he said, and hung up on her.

Ana dealt with the courts for years. She heard every excuse ten times over, and it never worked on her. She knew he was lying, so when he walked in the office a half an hour later, she wasn't surprised. She didn't even bring up the lame excuse he tried. They went right into discussing his alcohol abuse and how it was ruining his life.

After work, Ana was troubled driving home. She kept thinking about Marcus. He would have been five when the war happened. He could not have been taken into LORE. They could not corrupt small children. His father was the one touched by darkness, so how did he pass it on to Marcus?

When Ana opened the front door her heart leapt. Peter was there.

"Peter," she yelled hugging him tightly. He kissed her cheek.

"I just got in," he said.

"You didn't have to come all this way," she told him.

"You needed me, so I'm here," Peter said, seriously.

Maggie was hugging Peter's leg.

"I see you have a friend," Ana said.

The three of them ordered Chinese food and sat, eating with chop sticks. They laughed and talked, never bringing up the war.

After the dishes were done and the kids were put down to sleep, and Ana put fresh sheets on the spare bed, the three gathered in the kitchen.

Levi pulled out the two hand drawn pictures to show them to Peter.

"I've seen pictures of this man," Peter said.

"Where were you at the time?" Ana asked.

"In Germany. I was following up a lead that took me to a psychiatric nursing home. There was a man there who they called Opa Fredrick. He had hundreds of drawings, all of this man. I didn't think anything of it at the time," he said.

"Did he have the mark on his hand?" Levi asked.

"Yes, but it had not been activated. It was the face only." Peter said.

"What information did he give?" Ana asked.

"Not a thing. He kept rambling on and on. I had a hired translator. He would talk about sparrows that would fly out the ground and then turn into black crows and dive back down into the ground," Peter said.

Ana gave Levi a strange look.

"What?" Peter asked.

"That actually did happen," Levi said.

"I purposely left it out of the information I put online," Ana said.

"But, why?" Peter asked.

"It was Brother Antonio's idea. That part of my dream came after the original part, the first part that I put online. Brother Antonio told me there would be people having the same dream. When people came out of the woodwork, we could ask them questions about that part of the dream. It was before I knew Levi," Ana explained.

"It was a very effective tool," Levi said.

"So what else did the man say?" Ana asked.

"He said the world existed as a separate entity. That outside the world there were doorways that existed throughout the universe. That beings of light and beings of darkness could come through the doorways," Peter said.

Ana interrupted him, "Angels and demons."

"Yes, that is what we call them. We are created from the light and the darkness. Most of us are a good balance of both. Some people have more light and some people have more darkness. LORE could easily sway the people who are made of more darkness, and could convince the people who are balanced that their way is the only way. However, they desperately desire the people who are made of more light. They will try to change people, to pull them to their side," Peter said.

"Where is God in all of this?" Levi asked.

"That's the interesting point, according to this old guy. God gave us his commandments and his Son, but leaves the path we follow to be our choice. The place that we saw is in space, but one side is good and the other is evil. The angels are the guardians of the good side, and the demons are the guardians of the evil side. But now, evil is breaking into our world through tears in the world," Peter said.

"But, we drove them back after the war againt Christian," Levi said.

"Yes, we did but they are stilling finding ways to come through," Ana said.

"It's just a story from a crazy guy," Levi said.

"I don't think so," Ana said. "It would make sense. As a people, we have such duality, always struggling within ourselves. We closed the dark teardrops by using the light that lives inside us. When I was in my dream last night, the closer those creatures got to me, the more excited they were. What does a man in the desert dying of thirst want?" Ana asked.

"Water," Levi responded looking confused.

"To live in the darkness all the time makes them crave the light," she said.

"Then why does the light close the dark teardrops?" Levi asked.

"Because it can't survive in the light, even though it wants to," she said.

"What about Christian? How could he survive in our world?" Ana asked Peter.

"Well, except for during the war, I never saw Christian out in the light. His room was always dark and the lights were low for any meetings we had," Peter said.

"Is this new man another Christiant?" Levi asked.

"I hope not," Ana said. "We barely survived Christiant, and we were a lot younger."

The two men laughed until they saw Ana was serious.

"Maybe he is the demon on the horizon. Either way, we will be ready," Peter told them.

"That's not enough," Ana said. "I don't want my children fighting demons. I want to make this a better world for them."

"Ana, we already have," Peter said, covering her hand with his. "Let's try to figure out how many tears there are in the dark. Then we can make a plan on how to close them."

"It's late. I think we all need some sleep," Levi told them.

Chapter Ten

Ana opened her eyes to find herself flying in a white gown. She was above White Fish Point, and seemed to be stuck there.

She looked around. What was she supposed to be seeing? She followed the light from the Lighthouse as it moved out on the water and then over the city.

She could not see anything unusual. Her eyes became tired trying to follow the light, so she looked just behind the light.

She was astounded by what she saw behind the light: many darker creatures running toward it. There were not too many of them, maybe three to four. The light blinded her for a second, and she sat up in bed.

Blinking her eyes, she finally could see around the room. Levi was snoring loudly, so she turned him on his side and, pulled the covers over herself. She slept peacefully the rest of the night, knowing that in the light of day the world always looked better.

She entered the kitchen the next morning, and found her children eating breakfast.

Dante moved oddly slow.

"Dante, finish your cereal," Ana said.

"Mom, a man came to see me last night," Dante said.

Ana's hand began shaking so badly, she spilled her coffee all over the floor.

"Levi," the sound barely escaped her throat. "Levi," she repeated, a little louder.

Peter and Levi entered the kitchen, saw Ana's pale face, her shaking cup, and ran to her side.

"Ana, it's okay," Levi said. "We're here."

She looked at him with her expression frozen. "He saw the man," she said, finally, as she set the coffee cup on the table.

Levi looked at Dante, and stooped down in front of him.

"Tell me what you saw," Levi said to him.

"He was a dark man in a black suit with gold buttons," Dante said. "He had a long black beard. I couldn't see him well, but he asked me about Maggie."

Ana's head dropped into her hands.

What did he want to know about Maggie?" Levi asked clutching the boy's arms.

"Dad you're hurting me," Dante said.

"Oh, my God, Dante. I am so sorry," Levi said picking him up in his arms. "It's just that this is very important. So tell me, what did he want to know about Maggie?"

Dante looked over at his mother and said softly, "He wanted to know how attached I was to her."

A dead silence fell over the room, and for a

moment, time stopped.

Finally, Levi breathed in deeply. "What did you tell him?" he asked.

"I told him that Maggie has the greatest light, and we won't let him have her."

Ana picked up Maggie protectively in her arms, and went into their bedroom.

Levi continued talking to Peter and Dante in the kitchen.

After a time, Levi went to see Ana.

Maggie was watching cartoons, snuggled up with her pink blanket in the middle of the bed.

Ana was running her fingers through Maggie's curly brown hair.

Peter and Dante came through the door behind Levi.

"Whatever happens, we will deal with it," Levi said to Ana.

She was looking off into space as if no one was there.

"It's the message," Ana finally said.

"What is?" Peter asked.

"I was given two messages. Walk in the light of the Lord and you will never know darkness. I thought it meant that if you were kind and good to others you were living in God's light," she said.

"So that's not what it means?" Peter asked.

"No, it has to do with the second message. The one that I never told anyone. The second message was 'In the purest part of the light, you will always find God'. The angels in our dreams were not symbols of what was to happen. They were physically real.

The message was, we should walk in the light of the Lord. Some people are almost all light and when we find those people, we need to stay with them so the darkness does not consume us. Last night I dreamed of the Lighthouse. We need to take the kids and go there," Ana said.

"How do we know who is made of all light?" Peter asked.

"How about Jesus? He was made of God and of light. We are looking for someone made of all light," Levi told them.

"Why do the two of you think there is someone made of all light?" Peter asked.

"Because we know two people made of all darkness," Ana said, "Christian and this new man. If they can exist in our world, then people made of pure light must also exist."

"How can we find them?" Peter asked.

"Maybe we don't have to," she answered.

Picking up Maggie, the five of them headed outside. They drove together to the Lighthouse. It was their first home together, and they felt some relief on returning. Walking up the circular white steps was a walk down memory lane.

"Your mom and dad met here," Peter was filling in Dante as they walked.

A young college guy was the new caretaker for the Lighthouse. Ana waved to him as they started up the stairs.

Ana handed Maggie to Levi when they were halfway up. As they stood on the observation deck, Ana said to Maggie, "Lets sing a song. 'This little light of mine, I'm gonna let it shine.' Can you sing with me?"

Maggie sang, "My light gonna shine."

"Good, Maggie," Ana said.

"Now I want you to hold your hand like this and make the light inside come out," she said.

Maggie held her hand up and a bright light came out of it.

Ana turned her slightly, and the light reached an area past downtown. They saw smoke rise out of a house as Maggie's light hit it.

"Dante, come to mom," she said. "Hold out your hand like Maggie, and try to bring the light out," she told him.

Dante closed his eyes and breathed deeply. The light came out as strong as Maggie's.

Levi picked up Dante, and they walked with the kids all the way around the Lighthouse. They cleared out the entire city of any darkness that existed.

"What now?" Peter asked.

"Now we have to figure out how to find people of the light, people who can see the light, and the dark teardrops," Levi said.

"I was touched by Christian's blood. That is why I can see the darkness and the light," Ana said.

"You mean we can see the darkness because we were exposed to it," Levi said.

"Why can the kids see the light and the darkness?" Peter asked.

"Kids can usually see things that grown ups can not," Ana said.

"What do you think the demons will do, now

that they know we can stop them?" Peter asked.

"Whatever it is, we will face it together," Levi said.

It was a warm and sunny Saturday, and Ana was determined to make the most of it. The kids played in the sprinklers outside, while Ana went back online. Her website was huge. Everyone posted comments.

It became an end of the world site. Many theories from the believable to the extreme were thrown around there.

There was a whole section called AD (After Detroit). It consisted of people who were converted to Christianity after Detroit's war, and stories of their conversions.

Ana had not blogged in years. She pulled up her personal blog on the site, and typed into the New Information section.

"This is not going to go well in the church," Ana said, "people made of darkness and light."

When Ana finished, she hit send and online it went. She asked for anyone who could see the light and or the darkness to get in touch with her.

A strange thought ran through Ana's head: was she recruiting an army?

Later, Ana pulled the kids in for dinner, and begged Peter to stay for a few more days.

After getting the kids ready for bed, Ana decided to put them in her room for the night. Thank goodness they had a king size bed, she thought.

She left them watching TV in bed, so she could clean up the kitchen.

Levi came to her side, and she bade Peter goodnight before going to bed.

Maggie had already fallen asleep, and Dante was struggling to keep his eyes open. He so wanted to see the end of his favorite show: "Duo in Denmark." It was a mystery show about two young guys.

Ana stroked his hair as he succumbed to sleep. She switched to a political show after she was sure he was sleeping.

Then she heard a noise. It was like a group of birds flapping heir wings. At first, it was no big deal to her, since they lived by the lake.

The sound changed to hundreds of birds flapping their wings.

There was a scream, and the sound stopped.

Levi and Peter came to her side.

"Tell me you heard that," Ana said.

"Maybe we were all asleep," Levi stated.

"No," Ana said. "I always know when I'm asleep. We were definitely awake."

"Do we have any weapons?" Peter asked.

"I have knives and an axe in the garage," Levi told him.

"No, don't leave the house. We need to stay together. We are stronger together. Get some candles. The light will protect us," Ana said.

Levi and Peter ran to the kitchen to get candles and whatever knives they could find. They brought the candles to the room and placed them all around.

Levi turned on all the lights in the house. He went to the front window and peered outside. There was suppose to be a fingernail moon, but even that was gone. All he saw was darkness.

Returning to the bedroom, he found Peter in a brown rocking chair with a large butcher knife.

Ana sat with a protective arm over the children, and with a large knife in the other hand.

Levi kicked off his shoes and sat on the bed with his family.

They heard a loud clap of thunder, and the electricity went off.

Luckily, Ana and Levi had invested in a backup generator, which kicked in within minutes. That seemed only to aggravate the creatures outside.

They heard loud clawing on the sides of the house and in the attic.

"It sounds like they are ripping the house apart," Ana said, covering her ears.

There was a loud bang as the front door burst open.

Levi jumped up and closed the bedroom door. He sat with his back against it.

The sound changed. It sounded like hundreds of birds were flying through the house.

There was a banging on the door and a deep male voice yelled, "We only want the children. Give me the children, and this will end now."

Peter reinforced the door with Levi.

Ana heard a cracking sound as the bedroom window gave way.

Hundreds of small black demons entered the bedroom. They got to Peter first, as he stood striking them with a large butcher knife. They covered him, ripping him to shreds. They opened the door and carried the pieces out of the bedroom.

"No!" Ana cried. She pulled her children closer to her, holding them as tightly as she could.

One of the demons hopped onto the bed, quizzically looking at Ana. It was so taken by her, it merely sat and stared at her.

Ana reached out and touched the small cold creature. After she touched him, he turned into a white dove, and flew out the window.

"Dante, Maggie, touch the black animals," Ana said. She was unsure what to call them, other than animals.

Ana stood on the bed, touching the little black demons, and watching them transform.

Their black beaks and long clawed feet were sharp. One scratched Ana across her face. She caught him in mid air and watched him change.

"Here, birdies," Maggie was saying. She would touch them, and they turned into snow white doves that flew out the bedroom window.

Levi was beaten, but alive.

When the last dove flew away, a silence ensued.

Ana started to go to her husband's aid.

"Stay with the children!" he ordered.

Ana moved back to the bed. Neither of the children were bitten nor scratched.

Ana kept thinking about what Peter said. The creatures of the darkness desired the light.

After a few minutes, Ana told Levi to put a dresser in front of the door. She took a picture with a wooden frame and put it across the broken window.

She went to the bathroom and wet some towels. She wiped the cuts on Levi's arms and face.   "What now?" she asked him.

"We have to leave, Ana," he said.

"Not again!" She had left her life before, because she had to. Looking down at Maggie, she knew they might not have a choice.

"When?" Ana asked.

"Sunrise," he replied.

Tears rolled down Ana's face.

She lost Peter. It had been a long time since she lost anyone.

They heard the sound again, like hundreds of birds flying.

Ana ran to the window to reinforce the picture with her hands.

Levi went to the dresser and looked in the bottom drawer. He came to Ana with nails.

"Where did you get those?" Ana asked.

"On our trip to Jerusalem. They are replicas of the nails used on Jesus," he replied.

He used the back of his butcher knife to pound the nails through the back of the picture, nailing it to the wall. As the nails entered the glass, they made a crackling sound.

Ana and Levi sat back on the bed with the kids.

"What's gonna happen now?" Dante asked.

"I'm not sure, but we are together," Levi replied, hugging him close.

Ana held the half awake Maggie in her arms.

"Birdies," Maggie said.

Ana stroked Maggie's soft innocent face lightly, as she fell back asleep.

"We closed the teardrops doorway," Ana said. "That's why they are coming after us."

Levi took her hand in his. They didn't need any words.

The attack was the great darkness that did not come seven years ago. The demons wanted Peter, since he was damaging LORE's ambitions.

Ana felt like a fool. She played into their hands.

All of a sudden the pounding started again.

Levi ran to the door and sat against it.

Ana pulled the kids closer to her.

The pounding stopped and they heard a familiar voice.

"They left. Let me in."

"It's Peter," Ana said softly.

"No way," Levi said. "It's not Peter,"

"Please guys, let me in," the voice said.

"We know it's not you," Levi yelled.

"Don't talk to it," Ana said.

The other voice responded. "Do you know what we wanted at Marcus' house? His sister. She was like Maggie and Dante," it said.

"So why did you need Marcus to kill them?" Ana yelled.

There was no answer.

"I know why you can't do it yourselves," Ana continued. "You can't survive in the presence of the light. In the purest part of the light, we find God. You can influence people, but you can't touch the light.

You took Jesus down to the darkness, but he rose and was resurrected," Ana yelled at the demon.

"All we have to do is open a small doorway and we can make you do whatever we want," the demon replied.

"Aaaghhh!" Levi screamed holding his right hand in agony.

"Levi," Ana cried rushing to his side. "What is it? Show me," she said.

Slowly, he opened his hand to see that the three red six's returned.

"That's not possible," Ana said. "You burned off the mark."

Levi picked up the butcher knife and looked at Ana. His eyes glowed red for just a second.

"Levi," Ana said backing away from him. "You are stronger than they are. Please fight this. I know you can," Ana said.

Levi was in a trance as he moved towards the bed and her two babies. He was fighting within himself.

Ana could see it. She moved closer to him and opened his fingers that grasped the butcher knife. She took the knife from him and threw it across the room.

In a single swift moment, he punched her on her left cheek.

She fell to the ground.

He climbed onto the bed.

Dante put his fist up to protect Maggie.

Levi threw him off the bed.

Ana jumped onto Levi's back to pull him

away.

In the commotion Maggie awoke, and with sleepy eyes looked up. "Hi, daddy," she said, touching his face.

The blackness suddenly came out of him, and disappeared in the light Maggie created.

Ana grabbed the knife and ran to the door. She swung open the door, and in a less than a second, pushed the knife into the chest of the man standing there.

The man pushed her back into the room.

As the man came at her, Levi held Maggie in front of him.

Maggie showed her hand to him.

He burned in the light from Maggie's hand.

Levi set Maggie on the bed, and sat beside her.

Ana rushed to him, crying. She grabbed him and held him tightly.

It was five thirty in the morning and the sun would be up soon.

They family lay together, and when the sun rose, they fell asleep together.

In the purest part of the light, we find God.

This is the Gospel according to Ana:

….WALK IN THE LIGHT OF THE LORD, AND YOU WILL NEVER KNOW DARKNESS.